What Readers Said About
A Gentile in Deseret
Believe in Love, Book 1

"I am having trouble doing housework or anything else since I received your book! Thanks and keep up the great writing." P. S., Washington

"What a great book. It is true that it is a Christian love story, but it also stands on its own as a really interesting, easy-to-read piece of young adult fiction. . .(it) does not come across as a book that is disrespectful to the LDS faith . . . Overall excellent book." B.R., Massachusetts

"This is a very well-written, easy to read and actually quite informative Christian love story. Rosanne Croft answered questions about the Mormon and Evangelical religions in this well laid out story (set in Utah) that I didn't even know I had. . .I liked it!" C. B., Florida

"Excellent book. I didn't want to put it down until I had read it all. I can't wait for her next book." K. P., Wyoming

"I loved this book and found it took me back to my high school years as a Gentile in Deseret. What a beautiful example of the real life culture I took part in growing up here in Utah . . . (written) in a non-attacking and graceful way. I am hooked on this series and anxious to get my hands on book number 2. I want one for sure!" S. M., Utah

"Just finished it . . . loved it and can't wait to read the 2nd!!" F. H., California

"For me, this was a cover-to-cover read! Excellent story of love, learning, and growing up." K. T., Utah

Believe in Love *Series*
Rosanne Croft

A Gentile in Deseret
Book 1

A Saint in the Eternal City
Book 2

For Time and Eternity
Book 3

A Saint in the Eternal City

ROSANNE CROFT

Grace in Jesus ~
Rosanne Croft
Galatians
2:19-21

ISBN-13   9780692661703
ISBN-10   0692661700
Library of Congress Control Number: 2016905169
Rosanne Croft, Redmond OR

Cover design 2016 by Lynnette Bonner.
Author photo by Ray Croft.

Printed in the U. S. A.

DEDICATION

For Elder W., Seeker of Truth

DISCLAIMER

A Saint in the Eternal City, Book Two in The Believe in Love fiction series includes ideas gleaned from observation, personal anecdotes, and years of research on LDS teachings. Names are randomly chosen, and any resemblance to living persons is purely coincidental. All Biblical references are in the New International Version.

Books by Rosanne Croft

Once Upon A Christmas, 2015, Shiloh Run Press;
An imprint of Barbour Publishing, Inc.

A Gentile in Deseret, 2014, OakTara Books
(Second updated Edition published by Author, 2016)

A Saint in the Eternal City, 2016
Published by the Author

Like a Bird Wanders, 2009, OakTara Books

1

MISSING UTAH

Alex Campanaro sank deep into his garden chair, brooding over a cup of dark roast coffee. Outside Rome, his family's villa reflected the sienna color of the sky this August morning, but the beauty of the ancient house and courtyard had little effect on his mood. Turmoil swept through him like splashing water in the nearby fountain, scattering chaotic drops in every direction. A sudden breeze ruffled the violet flowers climbing the pergola, as well as his wild curly hair. Pumping with energy, he jumped up to pace the cobblestones.

His heart was back in Utah with the girl he loved. How he missed his blue-eyed blonde, Jennalee Young. Their goodbyes at high school graduation resounded in his mind whenever he glanced at her senior picture on his new cellphone. The loss of her pervaded his mind.

She'd told him, "I guess we set ourselves up for hurt like this when we started going out. It's all so impossible." *I'll say impossible.* Jennalee was right; dating a Mormon girl when he was a sold-out born-again Christian meant obstacles, lots of them. After she'd said it, he'd made a vain effort to quiet her crying.

"Don't look at it like that. One year, remember? We'll be back together in a year. I'll email you, I promise." A promise he couldn't keep since all their plans to communicate were a tangled mess. The pact to meet in a year fractured. Would he ever see her again? Had she totally forgotten what they'd studied in the Bible and gone back to her LDS roots? Maybe she didn't want him to find her.

On impulse before leaving for Italy, he'd sold his expensive smart phone to buy a plane ticket, unaware he couldn't relay his new number to her, since her number had also changed. Her parents succeeded in taking over her Facebook account, which she hadn't seen in three months as far as he could tell. All emails had gone unanswered. The Young family circled the wagons around their daughter, blocking him out.

He had to find her, talk to her, but how could he leave his demanding new job in Italy to go back to Utah? Just then his younger brother Gabe popped outside in his bathrobe, interrupting his worries.

"Hey bro, have you seen my camera?" he asked, squinting in the rich light. "I have to pack it for the trip back to Utah tomorrow."

"Sorry, Gabe, I meant to return it. I took some pictures of a client's vineyard, so it's still in the car."

Gabe perched himself on the edge of the table. "Why do I have to leave Italy to go to stupid ninth grade? Wish I could stay here and help in the wine business."

"You're the class algebra whiz. All your friends need you. Anyway, Mom says you'll both be back for Christmas. You know I have to stay." His summer job had extended through grape harvest. Maybe longer.

Gabe smiled, swiping his straight hair out of his eyes. "All summer without a haircut! It's driving me crazy." He hesitated. "When I get back, I'm getting a job because I need. . ."

"Money, right?" Alex guessed. His own job paid enough to save for college, and his dream of medical school.

"I need money so I can buy you a new laptop."

Alex walked over and put his arm around his younger brother. "Gabe, it could've happened to anyone. We had so much stuff on the plane to keep track of, and Uncle Lucio lent me a laptop for work, so don't worry about it, okay?"

Since their father died three years ago, Alex had more patience with Gabe, but in reality, the pain of losing the laptop unsettled him; another blow to his interrupted life with Jennalee.

"I'll go to the vineyards with you today," Gabe said. "I can take pictures while you talk business."

"It's a long day in the car, dude," Alex answered. "But Uncle Lucio's letting me borrow his midnight blue Maserati. We could try it out on the open road to Orvieto. Ask Mom, okay?" He anticipated driving the modern highway leading to Orvieto, a good workout for a powerful car.

Revitalized by a thought, he walked toward the stone villa, adrenaline flooding his body. "Never, never, never give up! Didn't Winston Churchill say it that way?"

"I think he said four nevers." Gabe looked smug.

"You brainiac, you *would* know that. Is Uncle Lucio in the kitchen? I need to ask for a few days off to fly back with you and Mom."

His brother grinned. "You're coming, too?" he squeaked. Gabe couldn't trust his voice not to go random and they both laughed.

Striding into the spacious country kitchen through the archway, Alex bumped into his uncle, carrying a tray of fresh croissants. One hit the worn wooden floor.

"I've got it," said his mother Gina, picking it up and wiping it on her skirt. She took a bite. "Can't waste even one of Nonna's home-made cornetti. She's been up since dawn making them."

Alex's grandmother, Luigina, whom they called Nonna, passed them carrying a tray of coffee, cream and sugar. She always wore a black dress and faded apron and this morning was no different. They all moved outside as Nonna set the tray on the long table under the vine-covered pergola where they ate every meal in the summer. His uncle and mother sat across from Gabe, who'd moved to a chair and spooned copious amounts of sugar into his coffee. Nonna darted back into the kitchen mumbling something about butter and jam.

Alex faced his uncle. "Uncle Lucio, I need a few days off to go back to Utah. There's someone I need to find." His mom clasped her hands in a prayerful way.

"Alessandro, of course, you should go home, but only for one week." His uncle was in a gregarious mood. "You work hard for me all summer; go settle your old life in America. Tell your crying girlfriends your job is far away. Ah, he does an excellent job, Gina. He knows how to talk to everyone, from owners to harvesters. And he has the most talented nose this side of the Tiber River. Our Alessandro knows wine, the life of Italy."

"*Grazie*, Lucio. He's a good son and you've taught him the business well." She took Alex by the arm. "You haven't reconnected with Jennalee yet?"

"I don't know what happened, Mom, but I've got to find out where she is." His mother's brow furrowed in deep thought.

"You have one special girlfriend, *sì?*" Lucio smiled a wide smile, showing a space between his white teeth. "I pay your way. Get married and bring her back to live here; the house is so empty since. . ." Lucio got emotional whenever he talked about his ex-wife leaving last year, taking his three daughters with her.

Alex covered up his own strong emotions with a dry laugh. His family in Italy wouldn't understand how hard it was to find Jennalee, much less marry her and bring her back.

"Thanks for offering but it's . . . complicated. Uncle Lucio, I can pay for the ticket myself."

"No, no, I transfer money to your account right away," said his uncle, running inside to his home office.

His mom looked puzzled. "I thought Jennalee went to college. Why hasn't she emailed you?"

"Our email doesn't work. She changed something, or her parents did. They sent her to Brigham Young University because they didn't want her going to Weber State with me."

"Alex, why didn't you tell me earlier you couldn't contact her?"

"You have your own problems, Mom, and when Carl came with us for the first two weeks, I . . . couldn't talk to you much. And this job . . ."

Their mother cleared her throat as if making a speech. "Boys, let's talk about Carl."

Gabe frowned, and Nonna left for the kitchen fussing about starting the day's sauce.

"Boys, I was impulsive when I invited Carl to come here. First guy I've dated since Dad died, and I thought it would be okay. He and your dad were friends when they were in the Air Force. But all along I noticed your discomfort and Carl's uneasiness, too. I think that's why he acted . . . cranky sometimes. After he went back, I had time to think, and decided . . ."

Alex locked eyes with Gabe. At least she knew they didn't like the guy.

"I'm going to give him one more chance. Carl's a Christian like we are, but sometimes he doesn't practice it like he should . . . and aren't we all subject to mistakes?"

Alex let out his held breath. She wasn't going to marry him. Not yet.

"So what do you guys think?"

"We want you to be happy, Mom," said Alex. "And . . . we don't want to say anything bad; we're just not sure he's the right guy for you, huh, Gabe?" His little brother nodded with tension, his foot wiggling under the table. The pain of losing their dad to cancer made Alex's voice stiff. He wanted to say more, but his throat constricted whenever the grief wound came back.

Their mom sighed. "I'm not totally sure about him either. But I do know I'm blessed to have you boys and my family here in Italy."

For Alex, the uncertainty hanging over them about Carl returned after months of forgetting about the grey-haired man back in Utah. Carl had his good points; he was a computer genius but everything he did seemed to be with himself in mind. He tried to be cool and young, cracking prejudiced jokes about Mormons.

Alex knew Carl's comments were flung at him because of Jennalee. But their mother didn't see his worst behavior, or didn't want to. Talking to Mom was harder after Carl came along, so he hoped she'd realize the truth about him. Alex had a strong feeling the man shouldn't be trusted.

Uncle Lucio came out with an envelope. Wiping away a tear, he said, "Here's some spending money for you and your brother. Gina, he is my best wine taster, like my own son, because you know I only have daughters. So God is good to bring him to me. I need this boy back soon."

"Stop complaining, it's only for a week, Lucio. At Christmastime, Gabe and I'll be back, too."

"And next summer," Gabe said. "Mom, can I go with Alex today?"

She nodded. "Get your clothes on, then. You can't go in a bathrobe."

Nonna breezed outside again to hand bagged lunches out to the boys and pick up empty coffee cups. What a grandmother! Alex knew her brisk manner would slow when the noon meal was over. That's when she loosened her traditional braided bun for a siesta on the couch in the living room. From the time he was a toddler, he remembered those siestas when everyone napped with fans whirring throughout the house.

"Okay, you two," said Mom, "be careful with Lucio's car. No speeding." Gabe hid a smile with his hand.

Lucio surrounded them in a bear hug, kissing the air behind their ears. He took Gabe aside. "This one, too, is like a son to me. Stay and help me, Gabriele."

"Stop, Lucio. You know Gabe has school and you have Alex until January when you have to let him go to college. He's a top student, and I don't want him to lose momentum, even if he's working for you through harvest."

Nonna took Alex by the arm with a strong grip, whispering in his ear. "*Sì.* Nonna, don't worry, I'll go to college, and then Gabe can take over the wine exports."

Uncle Lucio perked up as he took a long gander at Gabe. "No, no, not yet," he said, "*un po' ingenuo.* In *inglese,* 'still wet behind the ears'."

■ ■ ■

Minutes later the brothers inhaled the visceral scent of saddle colored leather seats and hardwood trim inside Lucio's sports car.

"I don't believe you get to drive a brand new Maserati, Alex," Gabe said on the road to Orvieto.

"I love driving this baby. With the export business just getting started Uncle Lucio wants to make an impression on our clients with it, so I get to drive it a lot."

"Wow, a teak dashboard. I've never been in a car like this before."

"I can appreciate it, believe me." Alex put his sunglasses on as the morning haze cleared.

"I'm going to miss the cousins coming over for Nonna's birthday during the harvest," Gabe said. "The whole family will be there with Uncle Giuseppe's boys and Lucio's girls, even Gisela." He sounded sad.

"Hmm, cousins crush?"

Gabe shook his head. "No way, I just get along with her the best. She knows English the best of all of them. Whoa, you took that curve fast."

"Testing the car. Wish you could try this car, Gabe. It handles like a dream."

"You know I don't have a license, even in Italy. Pay attention, you're scaring me."

"Hey, I'm slowing down; here's the place we need to be." He took a right on a long road lined with cylindrical cypress trees. The light over the vineyard was hazy, like one of Leonardo da Vinci's paintings. This mistiness blurred distant objects until the mountains he saw through his windshield looked exactly like they'd been painted by Leonardo. Ah, Italy, he thought.

After a couple hours, the friendly owners agreed to export their wine to America and signed a contract. The brothers got into the car for home when Gabe pulled out a sandwich.

"Wait a minute, you can't eat inside this car. This isn't my old truck, you know."

"Okay, okay. Pull over then and I'll get out. Aren't you hungry?"

He was, so they stopped on a dirt road between a vineyard and olive grove. Eating Nonna's chubby sandwiches under the hot afternoon sun, they talked about Utah while the scent of ripening grapes permeated the air with end-of-summer sweetness.

"I'm glad you're coming home with us, Alex."

"Me, too, but I'm worried about leaving this job. I'll have double the work when I get back, but it'll be worth it all if I find Jennalee."

The cypress tree shadows lengthened as they headed back in the Maserati. Gabe flipped through the pictures he'd taken that day. He suddenly stopped.

"Wait a minute. These are from last week when you had the camera. Who's the woman with you?"

Alex felt his face flush red. He tried to sound nonchalant. "A client's wife wanted pictures, so I went along with her. It's a big contract."

"She's hot, Alex, I mean for an old chick. Isn't she like, Mom's age or something?"

"Probably, but she and her husband are worth millions."

"She's kind of creepy. Want me to delete them?"

"Sure, I sent her the one she wanted. Don't worry, I can handle this. She's harmless, and I almost have their contract in the bag."

He stomped on the gas pedal to pass a delivery truck. Alex didn't want to talk to his little brother about Caprice Putifaro, the woman who met him like a cat about to pounce whenever he went to talk business with her husband.

2

PILGRIMS ON THE EARTH

Twenty-eight hours later, Alex woke up grumpy when their plane landed in Salt Lake City with a thud. Long transatlantic flights tested his ability to do without sleep. No matter, he needed to find Jennalee, and help his mother and brother resettle into the boxy rented house in suburban Kaysville.

"I guess we're home," Gabe said when the airport taxi dropped them off at their house.

Alex snickered. "You don't sound happy. Maybe it's because a day and a half ago you were in a Maserati Ghibli driving the hills of Italy."

"This place doesn't . . . feel like home and never will."

Their mother fished for her house key. "You're so right, it doesn't. We're only pilgrims passing through." She sounded forlorn, Alex thought, not at all like her old self.

After hauling luggage, the boys plopped on the couch. To Alex, the musty smell of the old house reminded him of high school days with his friends. Was it already a year since they'd moved to Utah and he'd met Tony, and then Jennalee?

"Let's pick the dog up at Tony and Eli's house. I missed Titus so bad." Gabe tore his shoes and socks off, and dug a pair of flip flops out of a backpack. "Where's the leash?"

"It should be in my truck."

Hungry, Alex checked the refrigerator. Messy ketchup bottles, half-used mayonnaise and other condiments lined the door, but no milk, eggs, or butter. He hated going to the store, but his mom was busy unpacking.

"Hey Mom, the students you subleased to didn't leave a thing in the fridge," he shouted into the bedroom where his mom played worship music as she emptied suitcases. "We'll go to the store and then get Titus."

The sound of his small truck's engine filled him with unexpected joy. The clunky old pickup was a far cry from the deep bass thrum of his uncle's Maserati, but he'd spent hours in it with his friends as well as taking Jennalee to school. A flattened balloon and tiny piece of mint green lace on the floorboards reminded him of prom and Jennalee, sitting there, breathtakingly gorgeous. He tried to hold on to this portrait in his head, not wanting to forget her, but at the same time he felt his old life fading.

Three months were gone and her alluring presence ebbed away, leaving empty foam like a wave when it goes back to the sea. He feared the mighty ocean of religion had succeeded in pulling her away from him. At BYU, she was probably back with Bridger, the guy she once said she detested. Her parents pushed her towards him but Jennalee resisted their pressure. Or did she? Was she even *trying* to contact him?

Gabe opened the passenger door. "I couldn't find it so I had to get another leash. Are you okay, Alex? You look tired or something."

"Jet lag's getting to me this time. *Andiamo*, let's go," he said with a sour smile.

In minutes, they pulled into Smith's grocery store, with the parking lot full of seagulls as usual, screeching over some cast-off food. The Great Salt Lake attracted the birds inland, where they were awarded rock star status of State Bird, because they'd saved the early Mormon pioneers' crops from devastation after eating an enormous plague of crickets. He hated the dirty scavengers, fighting over bits of run-over French fries.

Gabe's flip flops whopped the linoleum as they went inside, annoying Alex, who felt the edge of a headache starting.

"Well if it isn't Alex Campanaro," said a familiar voice. "Oh my heck, I haven't seen you since graduation." It was Madeline Silva, waiting near the entrance for her mom to check out.

"Hey, how's it going?" Alex felt genuinely happy to see her. "I have a job in Italy but I'm back for a few days."

Gabe got a cart and headed for the snack aisle as Madeline chattered on about going to Weber State with her boyfriend. Alex and Jennalee were supposed to go there, too, but none of those plans had worked out. So it was hard to listen to the peppy Madeline, who had none of the obstacles he faced.

Especially when she asked, "So you and Jennalee broke up?"

Should he tell her about their secret pact to reunite after a year? He thought not.

"No, we're just taking a break. I have a great job in Italy, and she's at BYU. Only, uh . . . Madeline, you wouldn't happen to have her cell phone number or email, would you?"

"You totally did break up then."

"We didn't break up. She changed her phone, and I changed mine, that's all." Drained, he wasn't up to a long chat on his romantic status.

"Oh, so you haven't heard from her all summer. Could it have to do with the returned missionary from BYU?"

Alex flushed with anger. "You mean Bridger Townsend. Far as I know, he's out of the picture." Maybe, he thought.

With a calm and cool face, Madeline glanced at her cell phone contacts. "I heard her parents were pushing for them to go down the aisle. You know how it is here. The wedding reception hall on Gentile Street is booked up every weekend. This week it's congrats for 'Travis and Leslie' and three other couples. I've been watching for names I recognize, but so far, nothing."

Alex coughed, annoyed at his non-Mormon friend even though she'd helped him when he'd just moved to Utah.

"Sorry, Alex, I don't have her number. Jennalee and I were never close, you know."

"Right." His eyelid twitched, signaling he was beyond tired.

"She always thought I was trying to make the moves on you, Alex."

"I guess she did. Well, thanks, anyway."

Madeline grinned suddenly. "I do hear from Corinne. Remember the little mousy girl sitting in the back of Chemistry class? I think she's from Jennalee's neighborhood ward so I could ask her."

"Yeah, I remember; she went to senior prom with a friend of mine. Tell her I need to talk to Jennalee before I go back to Europe in a few days."

"Okay, I'll message her right away. You look terrible, Alex."

"So I'm told. Hey, thanks Madeline, not for saying I look terrible, which I already knew, but for trying to find Jennalee. You're a good friend."

She smirked. "A little sleep and you'll look as handsome as ever. Jennalee must have been crazy to let you go."

He shrugged. After they exchanged cell phone numbers, he caught up with Gabe who'd piled up a cart with his favorite snacks.

"C'mon, Gabe, get the real food so we can pick up Titus. Did you get dog food yet?"

■ ■ ■

Tony Morris, his best friend, had contracted a summer job on a fishing boat in Alaska and he wanted to hear about it. He'd met Tony in church youth group with Pastor Ron. Tony had stuck by him last year through all his efforts to go out with Jennalee, even though he'd warned Alex about dating a Mormon girl.

He pulled up and their dog Titus ran to the metal gate, tail wagging. Gabe rushed out to him, opened the gate and hugged his neck, red Chow fur flying. Tony's brother, Eli, who was watering roses, put the hose down and helped Gabe gather the dog's bed and belongings.

Alex got out of the truck and got Titus inside the cab, as Tony swaggered outside drinking a can of root beer. "I can't believe it. Mr. Italy is back without his Maserati."

Alex smiled. "Yeah, it's me for a few days."

"Thought it'd be just Gabe and your Mom."

"I came to see Jennalee." No time to explain the whole story.

"Didn't think it was for my sake." His friend put on a dejected look.

"You're an added benefit. Here's what we men do in Italy. . ." Alex hugged his friend, hands on his shoulders, kissing the air behind each ear.

"Tony, I mean it; it's awesome to see you. I'm glad you're back in one piece, and with lots of money."

"It wasn't too bad. Nice money, enough for the first year of college and then some. Only needed stitches once." Tony showed Alex his ankle.

"What happened?"

"Tripped over a bunch of nets . . . even after I got my sea legs."

"How many stitches?"

"Twelve, but after I got used to the whole weird world, I had an awesome time, made friends, caught a lot of fish."

"You make friends wherever you go, Tony. I sure wish I could stay, but I've got a humongous headache and groceries in the car. Can you come over and hang out day after tomorrow?"

"Drinking too much Italian wine, huh?"

"No, jet lag. And FYI, I never drink too much wine."

"Whoa, so serious. I haven't told my parents about your wine merchant job. I didn't say anything because they might think you're a bad influence. I mean, we're underage."

He was too tired to talk about it. "Well, they can't help it, they're not Italian. See, our blood is partly fruit of the vine." The comment reminded Alex that many evangelicals along with Latter-day Saints thought drinking any alcohol was a serious sin.

Tony nodded. "I believe you. Hey, we could crash Pastor Ron's house for Worship Night tomorrow. Can you make it?"

Alex shrugged. "I'm not sure. It depends if . . ."

He couldn't commit, too pressed to find his girl. His previously fiery faith must have slipped because there was a time when he wouldn't have missed praise and worship. He couldn't think about it, telling himself his focus had to be centered on making money in the wine business. His Bible reading slipped and without Jennalee sharpening him with her questions, he was faltering and knew it.

Tony whistled. "Man, you look terrible. Long flight, huh?"

"You're not the first to tell me. *Ciao.*"

■ ■ ■

"Better get the mower out, Gabe." They were watching Titus bound through the long grass in their backyard. "Those students never mowed the back."

He went inside to unload groceries. As he reached for another bag, the doorbell rang.

"Hello, young man," said Carl, through the screen door, "I didn't know *you* were coming." A look of surprise appeared behind his false smile.

"I'm only here for a few days. C'mon in." Then he shouted, "Mom! Carl's here to see you," just as Gabe revved up the noisy mower.

"Sorry, I'll go get her. Can I get you something to drink?" Alex asked.

"How about some of the famous Giovanini wine? Bring any back?"

He didn't like Carl's mooching attitude. "No. We just bought some Pepsi, though." Carl couldn't expect wine in the afternoon without a meal, could he?

"Pepsi? Drink it and you'll end up in outer darkness." Carl laughed without mirth.

"I've heard that." For some reason, in Utah, Coca-Cola was sold everywhere and Pepsi was hardly ever offered by restaurants. He didn't know why.

"So why is Pepsi an act of treason here anyway?"

"Because," said Carl in a superior way, "LDS business conglomerates bought big stakes in Coke, so the faithful are encouraged to buy all Coca-Cola products."

"I see, and boycott Pepsi while they're at it. So why do we care? We're not Mormon."

"Right, Alex, we're not Mormon. In Utah, there's an unspoken tradition that we stay away from them and they keep away from us. At least, that's the way it should be."

Another dig. His attitude made Alex's head ache more. Fuming, he left Carl on the couch and went to the kitchen to fill up a glass with ice for his Pepsi.

His mother came up from the basement where she'd put away the empty suitcases. Alex only had to glance toward the archway leading to the living room for her to spot the visitor on the couch.

Her face unreadable, she took the iced Pepsi to Carl, greeting him with a kiss on the cheek. Alex didn't want to hear any conversation so he skipped out the back door and grabbed the mower from Gabe, who looked at him like he was crazy. Zipping through the front and back lawns, he dumped three bags of clippings on a tarp in the driveway and finished in less than half an hour.

Gabe helped him bag it up. "What are you? The energizer bunny?"

"I didn't want to be inside."

"I can see why. Carl already? I mean, we just get home, and he shows up." He shoved grass in a black plastic bag with gusto.

"Yeah, it's him, in his controlling mode. Let's hope Mom sees him for who he is."

"We need to tell her what we *really* think of him, Alex."

"She'll figure it out; Mom's smart that way. We shouldn't get involved."

Minutes later, Alex and Gabe heard raised voices on the front porch. They went back inside the house and listened through the open screen door.

Mom's voice rose an octave higher than when she argued with her brothers in Italy. "How could you? It was none of your business. You took something important from my son and played God. Who do you think you are?"

"I only did it for you, Gina; you were so worried about the whole thing. I mean, she's a Mormon! I've lived in Utah for years and I know all about them. Pete never would've wanted his son to end up with a Mormon."

"How dare you? Leave my husband out of this."

"I'm sorry, Gina, but I know I did the right thing."

"Of all the self-righteous acts I've seen, you take the cake. I shouldn't have trusted you about my concerns. My son, even if he's young, has a right to make his own life decisions."

Alex gritted his teeth and waited for Carl's answer.

"I prayed about it, and maybe I intruded, but as you know, God works for the good." Carl didn't back down even after being yelled at by a mad Italian woman. He knew his mom; the fury in her waving arms and rapid fire Italian. Or English, as the case may be.

"When has God ever allowed us to lie and cheat for what we think is a good end? Tell me if that's in your Bible, Carl, because it's not in mine."

"Lying? I didn't lie." At this, Alex started for the door to help his mother. Gabe grabbed his arm, whispering, "It's between them. You said we have to stay out of it."

Thunder came from Mom's voice. "You've not been honest with me from the beginning. I had to find out for myself about your addiction to gambling." She paused. "I see by your face, I'm right."

Alex shook his fists in the air. They stayed clenched as he paced the floor to keep himself from walking outside to wallop his mom's sometime boyfriend. Gabe watched him, his eyes round.

The couple continued to argue. "Gina, I was going to tell you everything after we got to know each other better and. . ."

"Too late, Carl. No matter who Alex 'ends up with' as you put it, I have to trust the Lord with his choice. You don't know him. Nor do you know his girlfriend."

Carl's voice could barely be heard. "I hoped we could make it work, Gina."

Mom's voice shook. "I had a faithful husband who died, but I still have two wonderful sons. And anyone who tampers with us can't be trusted. You'd better go now." She came back inside the house, slamming the door with a bang. Then she walked into the tiny kitchen to face her boys.

Alex said, "Carl messed up my email with Jennalee, didn't he?"

"He admitted it when I told him I suspected him."

"You suspected him? How?"

His mother quieted. "I just know Carl. He won't admit he's wrong; he's been that way a long time. Stubborn."

"Remember the day he fixed my laptop; made it faster? He did it then, didn't he?"

Gabe said, "Yep, right here in the kitchen; you were doing the dinner dishes, and gave him your password. He did it right under our noses."

"Why would he do this to me the day after graduation? I never heard from Jennalee after that. And all this time I blamed her parents."

Their mom explained, "He changed her address and opened another account. She had one of those addresses with lots of numbers and letters so he changed one symbol, and that was it. The mail went into this false account, and he . . ."

"What a control freak. What'd he do, get off on reading my personal email? I feel so judged, Mom. Carl doesn't recognize that Mormon or not, Jennalee is closer to Jesus than anyone thinks!"

Mom sat down at the tiny kitchen table. "I'm so sorry, son. Carl thought he was helping me. I opened my mouth about my fears to him instead of trusting the Lord. I guess he tried to win points with me for solving my worries."

"Carl doesn't like Jennalee because she's LDS, plain and simple. But what I know about Christianity is: it's about loving people. And I love Jennalee."

"I'm sorry, Alex, I've put you in a difficult spot. I never should have confided in him about your personal life. I understand your anger, but don't make anybody your enemy."

"Carl makes me so mad," Gabe added, "remember how he was bragging on the tour of Aviano Air Force Base when we went to see where you and Dad met? He thought he knew everything."

"Now, Gabe. On his behalf, Carl did work with us there," said their mother, "but you're half right, he was bluffing because he wasn't popular. Your dad was kind to him, though. Always."

Alex sat down on a kitchen chair. "Mom, I'm kind of glad this came out. We were worried you might end up with him."

"So you had worries about *me*," she said, tearing up. "Come to think of it, when he left Italy, I felt like myself again. Guys, he's out of our lives but we have to forgive him and move on."

"How should we do that, Mom?" Gabe asked. "Look what he did."

"You can't judge until you know a person's story. Carl's bitter and hurt about being a total outsider here in Utah."

"That's no excuse for what he did," Alex answered, his hands forming fists. "He's self-righteous and crushed us just when Jennalee was learning about the real Jesus. I don't know if I can get her back now."

"I'm so sorry, Alex," Mom whispered, "God will straighten Carl out, as we keep our attitudes forgiving."

"Well, it's going to take me a while."

"No doubt." Then his mom changed the subject. "Well, Alex, what's the next step to pursue the girl you love and patch things up?"

"Carl got his way, Mom, because I have to find her first. I don't know where she is, so I'm planning to talk to her parents tomorrow."

"If I can do anything to help, I will. My life verse is Romans 8:28, 'And we know that in all things God works for the good of those who love him, who have been called according to his purpose.'"

Gabe's voice was louder than usual. "Did you hear Carl twist Scripture to what *he* thought was good?"

Their mother nodded. "Honey, people use Scripture to justify their wrong motives in all kinds of ways. But the deeper truth is that God *is* going to work this out, and if it's for the best, he'll bring Alex and Jennalee back together."

Alex's anger and hurt melted. He swallowed. "Thanks for that, Mom." The three of them hugged; weary world travelers home the first day.

3

THE SEARCH FOR JENNALEE

Morning light peeked through the curtain of his tiny bedroom and Alex resented it, squeezing his eyes, shutting it out. In his deep sleep, he'd forgotten where he was and when he remembered, a feeling of half dread and half excitement flooded his soul. Today was the day to visit Jennalee's house and ask for her contact information. It wouldn't be easy to see her disapproving parents, but his desire to find her outdid any fear of them.

In his truck, Alex listened to K-LOVE radio and along with his coffee, the music buoyed his courage as he parked around the corner from the Young house. He thought he'd pretend he was just walking by without any intentions. He didn't see her car; she probably had it in Provo.

On the last day of August, school hadn't started yet so three of her youngest brothers played basketball outside in the driveway. They stopped dribbling as he approached.

"Hi, Boston, remember me? Hey, Logan, Jordan. Where's Cade?"

"Mom took him to a dental appointment." Boston, at age thirteen, looked wary.

Alex tried to sound casual. "Well . . . I happened to be in the neighborhood and a while back I lost your sister's phone number. Can I get it from you?"

Logan spoke up. "Mom and Dad don't want us to talk to you." He dribbled the ball a few times for emphasis.

"Why not?"

"Because you're not LDS and you've interrupted. . . I mean interfered in our family," said Jordan.

"I know that's your mom and dad think, so what do *you* guys think? I've been a friend of your sister's for a year. I really care about her."

Jordan blinked at Boston, who stuck out his chest, arms dangling at his sides, in a tough stance. "It's none of your business where she is."

Helpless against the wall the Young brothers constructed against him, Alex took a step backward. "We used to hang out and play basketball, remember? Why are you doing this to me?"

Boston turned his head, but Jordan inched close enough to say, "She's in Provo."

"I know, at BYU, so do you have her number? Listen, I'll come back when your parents are here. I'm not afraid to ask them."

"Don't come back," said Boston, his voice tense. "Mom and Dad are mad at you. Mom's going to show up any second, so you better go."

"I don't care if you guys don't help me, I'll find her."

Logan dribbled fast. "Jennalee's . . . well, we had a big send-off for her."

"You better go now, Alex." Boston edged next to Logan and Jordan, forming a stalwart gang against any outsiders without the right credentials. Alex had no temple recommend, no badge to prove his worthiness to date their sister. Nonmembers and their ideas were threatening; he faced it before.

He nodded and walked back to his truck. No sign of Mrs. Young's car. Would she give him her daughter's phone number? He doubted it; her parents had changed it in the first place. With no other plan except to go to BYU and find her himself, Alex drove south on the interstate towards Provo. He thought about the last words Logan had said. A send-off? What did that mean? To send her off to college?

An hour later, the sheer size of Brigham Young University with residence halls, apartments, and thousands of students overwhelmed him. He hadn't planned this search and knew he should've strategized before he came. But since he was here, Alex decided to ask at a dorm or two.

In one of many Heleman Residence Halls, a young woman at the desk said, "You mean Jeanine Young? I have seven Youngs listed, the closest first name is Jeanine. Is that what you said?"

Reality washed over him. The Young surname was numerous as the stars in Utah because Brigham Young had so many wives and children. Finding her would be way harder than he'd anticipated. He shook his head and walked out.

On the bulletin board near the door, he spotted a large sign saying: *Questions? We can answer them. Call a BYU Operator.* Relieved, he put in the number.

"Jennalee Young? One minute please."

He waited, itching to hear her voice. She'd say, "Alex? Is it really you?" She'd be so happy . . .

The operator rebounded. "I'm sorry, there's no Jennalee Young listed as a student at BYU. Are you sure she's here?"

"Yes . . . well, I don't know for sure, but I think so."

"Do you have her middle initial?"

"Yes, it's 'E' for Eliza. After Eliza Snow, one of Brigham Young's wives, you know."

"Uh . . . I see, just a sec."

He prayed a quick '*Help me find her, Lord*', as the operator returned with, "Sir, our records are precise. She's not registered as a student this semester. Could it be the Missionary Training Center you want?"

"She never wanted to go on a mission; she wouldn't do that!"

A heavy pause filled with an unnamed emotion floated through the phone. "Well, sir . . . the MTC has a separate number. I can give it to you; however you can't talk directly with missionaries-in-training. I'm sorry sir, anything else I can do for you?"

"Um . . . no, thanks for looking." He heard the quick click of the operator escaping him.

Now hungry, he stumbled into the Commons at Cannon Center and lined up to fill a plate high with chicken fajitas. The cashier looked him up and down in his jeans and faded Nike T-shirt.

"Student ID number? Card?"

"Sorry, uh. . . I'll pay cash." The cashier nodded, and acted relieved.

No doubt the relief stemmed from recognizing that he wasn't a BYU student and wouldn't need to be reprimanded for underdressing and not cutting his hair. He finished his lunch with no one paying much attention to him, until a portly girl sat in the chair next to him. The girl smelled like hair spray, a scent that rippled through his sensitive nose, stifling him with a chemical trail. He knew for certain he was the only sommelier on this campus and it almost made him laugh.

"Hi," the girl said, flashing a whitened smile, "you're not a student here, are you? Just visiting the campus?"

A loud sigh slipped from him. "How can you tell?"

"Your hair covers your ears and guys have to shave every day here. They're strict about the rules for us students."

Alex couldn't help it; his hand went to feel his two-day stubble. "Yeah, I do know." He stood up with his tray, feeling his ears warming under his hair.

"You're right, I don't belong here; I don't even *want* to be here." He tossed his garbage into the bin, and slammed the tray on top of the trashcan as the girl looked around anxiously to see if anyone had seen her talking to such a rude foreigner.

Sitting alone outside, the same feelings overcame him from a year ago; to be marked as an outsider in Utah was hard. In Oregon, he had more friends than he could count. The pervasive religion in Utah affected him so much, he could never feel at home here without Jennalee. Maybe the Lord was training him to be stronger in knowing exactly what he believed, but he still felt lost.

He needed to put self-pity aside and concentrate on his goal. And when he did, an idea popped up. Most of Jennalee's friends were going to BYU that year, so if he could remember their last names, he could call them. One name he couldn't forget: Bridger Townsend, the Young's preferred boyfriend for Jennalee. He redialed the BYU Operator service.

"Yes, I have a Bridger Townsend listed as a student. Would you like the number?"

He wrote it with a stub of a pencil on a receipt in his pocket.

So Jennalee and Bridger were students down here together. Maybe engaged, maybe even married. He pictured Jennalee throwing a bridal bouquet behind her shoulder after her wedding reception. Wasn't that a send-off? He shook his head wildly. She wouldn't have done it, would she? She would've run away first.

Bridger's number burned a hole in his pocket. Maybe he was the reason why she'd disappeared and hadn't been able to face him. Wrestling with intense jealousy, Alex remembered a Scripture to cheer him into action. *You shall know the truth and the truth will set you free.* As bad as it could be, he had to find out.

Fingers shaking, he punched the number and pressed TALK. It rang, and then a click with a taped message played. He listened to a generic message, complete with a robotic voice with Bridger filling in only his name.

Then the phone picked up and a woman's voice said, "Hello?"

His heart thumped but it wasn't Jennalee.

"Hey, this is Alex Campanaro." He closed his eyes and took a deep breath.

"It's you," said the woman. "Do you know who this is?"

"Nicole?" This was Jennalee's friend from high school, the one who never liked him.

"Yeah, it's me. Bridger's not here. I stopped by to put some of my famous chocolate cookies on his doorstep and heard the phone ring."

"He leaves his door open?"

"What business of it is yours? What do you want? Hurry up, Alex, before he comes."

"I'm looking for Jennalee." He was sure Nicole knew where she was.

"Oh, her. Lucky for you I answered this. Don't call this number again; Bridger pretty much despises you."

"I know, only we were friends once, remember, Nicole? So do you know where Jennalee is?"

"Yes."

"Okay, then? I don't have time to mess around."

"She's in the Missionary Training Center. She leaves in a couple weeks, because she's been there since . . . like, late June."

"Did you say . . .?"

"Yes. No one can see her, not even her parents. Missionaries have no personal phones. She gets email through MyLDSMail, but I don't know the rest of the address."

"I see." Alex felt dazed.

"I would've liked to help you even though she and I weren't speaking when she left."

"You weren't?"

"She hurt Bridger so bad, I can't even tell you."

Alex felt his numbness turn into keen awareness. "Well, thanks, Nicole, and congratulations!"

"What?"

"Aren't you and Bridger together?"

"We will be soon. Bye," she said, "and don't ever call back here."

He set his GPS to the nearby MTC. Pulling into the parking lot, he knew it was as close to an impregnable fortress as you could get, but he felt helplessly drawn to the one girl he wanted in his life forever. His imagination kicked in and he thought about crashing the gates and carrying his princess out. But he knew such imaginings were fruitless as he sauntered into the lobby, where two older women at the info desk explained what he already knew.

Then he remembered what Logan had said. "Can I ask you ladies a question? What's a send-off?"

One of the women laughed out loud while the other explained, "A family gives a send-off to their missionary by having a party before they enter the training center. It's like a *bon voyage* because they don't see them again for sometimes two years. Calls home are allowed twice a year, Christmas and Mother's Day."

Dejected, he got into his truck. Inside this prison Jennalee breathed and he couldn't break her free. She'd told him distinctly she wasn't interested in going on a mission; her dream was college and travel. Had she switched back to being fully LDS?

Was she covering up misgivings about her faith, the ones she'd talked about with him? He knew a mission counted for extra points in a religion where high performance mattered for earning heavenly rewards. With intense LDS training and knowledge drilled into her, would she ever be the same?

As he drove the congested freeway north to Kaysville, his old truck's exhaust contributed to the thick summer smog blanketing the valley. An inversion covered the valley with polluted air and to his sensitive nose, it smelled poisonous. Loads of small children were having asthma attacks tonight, he thought.

■ ■ ■

From his driveway, homey smells from his mother's kitchen enticed him from the open screen door and he breathed easier. Everything was so different after his dad died, but Mom's cooking would always be dependable.

"Here you are, bambino," said his mother as soon as he came inside. Seeing his face, she hugged him. "You didn't find her? Any leads?"

Home with his mom, his pent-up emotions broke loose. "She's a missionary locked up in the training center; she might as well be a nun in a convent. How could she have joined? We were supposed to meet next May."

"That's a long time, honey."

"You know *War and Peace*? We made a one-year pact like Prince Andre and Natasha. A year was long enough, but now she's stuck in a mission for eighteen months, so I guess she doesn't *ever* want to be with me."

"Surely you can reach her somehow, Alex."

"I'm trying to. The only good thing is she didn't marry that jerk, Bridger."

"At least she's not in love with someone else."

"It isn't a guy taking her away from me. It's the LDS Church."

His mom blew some air. "Well you can't solve it on an empty stomach. Made your favorite: chicken *parmesano con capellini, salata,* and *tiramisu.* Gabe went over to a friend's so we'll save him a plate."

Alex smiled for the first time all day. "Wow, Mom, you outdid yourself. Are you corking the Syrah we've been saving?"

"*Sí.* I guessed right, then, master sommelier, to choose Syrah for this meal. It's chilled and corked," she said, grabbing a wine bottle from the counter and pouring it into two glasses. "Wish Lucio was here to taste this Washington wine. Oh, I forgot."

"What?"

She laughed a little. "In America, it's against the law for you to drink this with me."

"You know what? Since you brought it up, Tony's parents think drinking wine is a sin for anybody. Mormons do, too."

Solemn-faced, Mom said, "Alex, I've said before I don't expect you two boys to follow my family's ways. Your American dad never touched a drop, for his own reasons."

"Wasn't his dad an alcoholic?"

"Yes, so Dad thought he should abstain. See, in America, people seem to drink . . ."

"Mostly to get drunk."

"Seems so," said his mother. "And you do see the damage it causes. On the other hand, Jesus drank wine and John the Baptist didn't, and they were both right. For them."

"I get it. You want it to be my own choice, right?"

"Study it out in the Bible, and I'll pray you neither fall under legalism nor under temptation to abuse it. Without self-control, just about everything is sin."

He loved his mom's answer, knowing her foundation was built from God's Word.

"Okay, but Uncle Lucio won't be too happy if I quit."

"No worries about him, honey, remember he's my little brother?" She held up a fist in the air and shook it, then picking up her wineglass said, "*Cent'anni.*"

Foregoing the wine, Alex picked up his water glass, and toasted, "May you live a hundred years, too, Mom."

■ ■ ■

Later that night, he called Tony. "Sorry I didn't make it to Worship Night at Pastor's. I was home with my mom."

"I take it you haven't seen Jennalee yet."

"Long story. We haven't been in touch all summer. I went to her house and her brothers stonewalled me. So I went down to Provo, and guess what? She's doing a mission. Not even her parents can talk to her."

"You're kidding, right? I thought she never wanted to do that."

"Tony, I flat-out don't know what to do. I feel ditched for the Mormon church."

"I hate to say this, but didn't I warn you?"

"Yeah," said Alex, "you did." But Tony couldn't understand his pain.

"Sorry, dude. I'll pray about the situation, but you need to talk to Pastor Ron."

"Can you get me his texting number? I have to go back to Italy in a few days and I might not have time to see him."

That hot summer night in his bed, he kicked off the top sheet. How could he love someone who broke his heart along with her promise? Jennalee had been the best part of his life, but in spite of his mother's comfort food, he felt acute pain when he pictured her. And Bridger still waited in the background unless Nicole snagged him with her cookies.

A text from Madeline relayed more of the same.

Are you vertical? Corinne says Jennalee's her roommate in the MTC. I'll try to get her email address for you.

Too late, he thought. Now it'd be another week or even two before he could reach her and by then he'd be back on his job.

Alex sat up in bed, shaking his sweat-filled hair in the heat of his room. He'd go back to Italy, where his life bloomed with success; where he drove a sports car, earned fat paychecks and enjoyed the *dolce vita* with his uncles and cousins. Nonna had even told him about a girl she thought would be perfect for him.

Still, no matter how he tried to drum up enthusiasm about his future, it was not to be conjured that last August night. A gaping hole of hopelessness rose up in his soul; a life without Jennalee. Dread, the feeling he'd awoken with, flooded back in as he went to sleep.

4

SEQUESTERED

In Provo, Jennalee closed her eyes amidst the clamor in the MTC cafeteria. The skylights let in minimal light, and the electric lights mounted along the walls couldn't make up for it. Like a mix between a hotel and a hospital cafeteria, the place was uncomfortable and public. Not like home. She stared at her plate, knowing her food was getting cold.

"Ciao, bella donna," Alex had said at graduation. That *'Bye, pretty woman'* proved to be his last words to her, his wild hair crowned with a mortarboard. Tanned face close to hers, he'd taken a selfie with his phone, although she'd never seen it. Nor had she ever seen him again.

In July, she mailed a letter to his Kaysville house, loaded with stamps, and hoped someone would forward it to him in Italy. Her parents could ever know how much she missed him. This 'snail mail' letter dropped into a postal box in Provo was her only chance to convey her new missionary email address. Two months passed and nothing from Alex. The letter must be lost somewhere in the giant machinery of the global postal service.

Reaching into her backpack, Jennalee removed her tattered copy of *War and Peace*. All she could think of when she read about Prince Andre and Natasha was they didn't have the overwhelming stumbling blocks to overcome that she and Alex had; at least they had the same religion.

"What're you reading?" Corinne, the friend she'd known since Primary at her local ward was now her MTC companion. Since Jennalee was assigned to the Madrid, Spain mission, and Corinne to Argentina, they shared Spanish classes.

"Just a book I picked up," she said in a breezy manner, slipping it under the table. "The entrée today is terrible; you're smart to stick with salad."

As soon-to-be missionaries, only LDS approved materials could be read while in the MTC and afterward, and Corinne would tell on her, she knew she would.

Her friend set down her tray. "Guess what I heard? Remember Brady and Shayna from high school? She's pregnant; they *have* to get married."

"I'm not surprised, Corinne."

Should she take the opportunity to set her friend straight on some hurtful gossip? Yes.

"To put any rumors aside, Alex and I aren't like that. We really do 'Choose the Right'." She automatically brushed the CTR purity ring on her finger.

"I would never think anything about you two." Corinne blinked a few times with her new contacts. She didn't act like the quiet girl from high school with glasses any more.

Jennalee said, "Well, I heard some rumors about us, so I want to get the truth out there." She checked for a reaction from her roommate and saw her blinking faster before answering.

"Speaking of high school, Madeline Silva messaged . . . uh, emailed me. She got a fantastic job with an insurance company plus she's going to Weber State with her boyfriend. He took her to prom, remember?"

Jennalee frowned. Corinne's mention of prom reminded her not of its wonders, but of its disastrous ending. An image of Bridger clouded her vision. He'd ruined the magical evening with Alex, and she'd never forgiven him.

"So, Madeline Silva resurfaces," she said, thinking how lucky Madeline was to live life the way she wanted to.

"And her boyfriend, Roy, you remember him. He's black."

"Nice guy. So?"

"I don't think he's LDS. No one I know has seen him at their ward chapels."

"Does it matter? Madeline isn't LDS either." The weary thought crossed her mind that for the umpteenth time, she played the game of trying to tell whether a person was or wasn't a member of the Latter-day Saints. Whether they did or did not 'belong'.

"Madeline likes Weber State but of course we know BYU is the best. She can't come here, being a Catholic. Well, she could, except for paying twice what we would pay."

Whatever happened to Corinne's shyness? She hadn't said a word in high school.

Jennalee changed the subject. "Are you coming back to BYU after your mission?"

"I don't know, I just want to find a guy and get married." Corinne grinned.

"Didn't you go to prom with Tony, Alex's friend?"

"Just the one date. It would never have worked with him."

"Why not?"

"He's not LDS. So have you heard from Alex yet?"

Jennalee swallowed. "No, but I'll be okay. Sometimes these things aren't meant to be." As Jennalee bluffed, she lowered her head lest her friend read her face. The last thing she wanted was this girl to know how she *really* felt.

Corinne's voice was breezy. "Contacting everyone whenever you want is the hardest thing to give up for the sake of the Lord. Too bad about Alex, though."

Jennalee retained her coolness, refusing to crack under subtle pressure. "I'll get over it." She knew she was playacting because though her friend seemed to genuinely care, she would never understand. For eighteen months she'd be tied up, unable to meet Alex in May. And he was in Italy working for . . . she could barely bring herself to think about it . . . his family wine business.

"I always thought Alex would make a great Mormon," Corinne said. "I mean he's so nice and I kind of wanted to see you two together. I guess it's not going to work out, but I still want to be a bridesmaid no matter who you marry."

"Right. I don't see a wedding happening any time soon. After my mission I'm going to college." Like she'd wanted to in the first place.

Even if she and Alex were able to talk, how could their high school love overcome physical separation? Religion had a way of standing between them since the day they'd met. If her parents ever knew about Alex's job as a wine merchant, they'd add layers of bricks to the wall they'd formed around her. But no one knew how determined she was to find him.

At first in their relationship, she thought Alex would become LDS, but it was Jennalee herself who now teetered on the edge of accepting his born-again Christian faith. Surrounded by the enthusiasm and holy purpose of hundreds of young LDS missionaries-in-training, she reverted back and forth in her beliefs daily, a dizzy see-saw in her head. But she kept reading the New Testament the way Alex had told her: like a child with no preconceived ideas.

■ ■ ■

That night, huddled in her bed, Jennalee, the 4th great grand-daughter of Brigham Young, put down her New Testament and cried hot tears of frustration, hiding them from Corinne. How she could pretend to have a testimony of Joseph Smith and the Book of Mormon when she secretly doubted it? Her brother Brent would never have unbelief like this. Not long ago, her tears were of heartfelt devotion to the LDS Church but tonight she cried from the deepest part of her spirit for the Jesus of the New Testament.

Worst of all, tomorrow she'd have to recite the daily mandatory public testimony.

"*I believe Jesus Christ lives and He is the Son of God, and carried out the Atonement.*" That part was easy, but the rest weighed her down.

"*I believe the Prophet Joseph Smith whom God called to restore the Church of Jesus Christ. I believe in the leading of the Lord's Living Prophet today. I believe the Church of Jesus Christ of Latter-day Saints is the only true church and the Book of Mormon is absolutely true."*

Jennalee keenly experienced how shaky her testimony was as she said it in class the next morning. Old rote beliefs rang hollow inside; she felt nothing as she said the words and a strange confusion took over.

She'd loved her childhood with her close and happy LDS family. Their lives were blessed with the financial success of her father's business and it was all because they followed the right religion, the one true church. At least she used to think so.

That was before she met Alex, who attended a non-denominational church. Although he loved being with God's people, he told her he didn't actually have a religion. The Bible was his guide and a foundation for his close relationship with Jesus.

Jennalee feared she could never be happy without Mormonism; it permeated every corner of her life. Then she'd think of Alex, strong in his faith in Jesus, even though he'd lost his dad to cancer when he was only seventeen. For her, whose foundations had always been the bricks of the LDS Church, the way he lived seemed almost too free, like a bird flying with no place to land.

She knew only to whisper prayers to a good and loving God that night, and a feeling of comfort welled up. Her choice to follow Jesus didn't mean she had to figure it all out. She remembered what Alex's pastor had said: "Just love Jesus, He'll do the rest."

■ ■ ■

Pasting on a smile the next morning for Corinne, she felt her happy façade faltering by afternoon. A messenger called her to the mission office. Filled with fear they'd found out about her doubts, she was loathe to say a word.

"You've been reassigned, Sister Young," said the clerk, "it's a rare occasion for missionaries to be reassigned at such a late date, however there's been an unfortunate incident whereby the previous Sister experienced a health crisis. You'll be sent to the Rome, Italy mission two weeks from now. You did mark Italian as one of your languages."

Italy? There could be no other explanation than God hearing her prayer last night. He'd answered with a miracle. She walked to dinner with Corinne, feeling tingly from the miraculous intervention of a God who heard and saw her tears even while sequestered in the MTC.

"You're awfully quiet. So what did they say? Something bad? Did they take the book you've been hiding?" Corinne blinked hard, her thin hair in wisps around her face. The poor girl had no drama in her own life, so she formed a habit of vicariously living other people's lives.

"Never mind the book. Sorry, I'm still processing. Corinne, you won't believe what happened, the Prophet reassigned me! So I guess I won't be in our Spanish class anymore."

"Oh my heck, what do you mean? We only have two more weeks. Where's your new assignment?" Corinne stared intently at her friend.

"Would you believe Rome, Italy? Where Alex is? I'm so happy I could scream."

Her friend got a puzzled expression on her face. "Are you sure he's there?"

Now it was Jennalee's turn to look surprised. "He's working in Italy."

Corinne shook her head. "Um. . . Madeline Silva says Alex flew back to Utah to find you. He's searching for you on the BYU campus . . . today."

Startled into silence, Jennalee felt sick. Alex had come to find her, but wouldn't be able to even see her.

"Corinne," she said, her voice jittery, "why didn't you tell me right away? When did Madeline say this?"

"Yesterday. . . I was afraid to tell you because you couldn't do anything about it anyway. And she thought you two had broken up for sure so I didn't think I should tell you."

In her head, Jennalee imagined herself reaching across and taking her so-called friend by the neck and shaking her.

"Did you even tell Madeline I was here in the MTC with you? I need her email address right away."

"Um . . . we have six more days before we can send messages. Madeline thought you were in classes at BYU and she told Alex. I didn't have a chance to say you were here."

"Now I have to wait six days for her address, with Alex outside looking for me."

Corinne shrugged. "Anyway, he won't be in the U.S. long, only a few days. Obviously it isn't Heavenly Father's will that you find him. His will is for you to go on your mission."

Jennalee her face get hot.

"Who are you to tell me God's will, Corinne? I'll miss Alex for weeks thanks to you."

Her voice cracked, she felt the verge of a meltdown approaching. In the pressure cooker of the MTC, lots of kids had emotional outbursts and she felt people around the crowded table starting to stare at her.

"Shh, Jennalee . . . I know I blew it. C'mon, let's go out in the hall."

Jennalee stood up, spilling Coke on the tray. "It's cruel, it's all too much. I may never see him again."

She stumbled out of the cafeteria. Corinne got rid of her tray and dishes and followed her to the restroom in the hall where she locked herself in a stall. An evening special musical program was about to begin, but she had to get away from the crowds of pumped up missionaries and the betraying presence of Corinne.

Her head leaned against the back of the door. For the next eighteen months of her life, another well-trained companion would be assigned to her constantly, always outside the door, waiting. How could she find Alex with a chain around her?

Then she remembered the miracle that had also occurred. Corinne was half right. Heavenly Father did want her to go on this mission, and if Alex flew all the way here to find her, she would find him in Rome. Finally walking out of the restroom, she stooped to touch her roommate's shoulder as she sat on the floor.

Corinne looked up, her hand to her ear. She was holding a phone!

"What?" Jennalee shouted, a little too loud. Seeing them, a hall monitor traversed the floor and grabbed the phone out of Corinne's hand.

"You know the rules, Sister. I'll have to report this to the office. Come with me, both of you."

Corinne, with a red face, peeked at Jennalee as they followed the MTC official. She whispered, "Now you'll have to give up the book you're not supposed to have."

"You lied," hissed Jennalee, "you've been talking to Madeline all this time."

"Maybe, but it was for your own good. You shouldn't go out with a non-LDS."

"I'll never trust you again, Corinne."

5

HOPE DEFERRED

Back in Italy, grape harvest was underway and Alex dug into his job with fervor, solidifying contracts before the season's new wine came in. It had been two weeks since he'd returned from Utah and there was no word from Jennalee.

With his usual morning coffee under the pergola, he checked his email. Autumn scents energized his sensitive nose: the rotting leaves, mushrooms, ripening fruit. His mother's note reminded him it was Sunday, and she sent him a link to an online church in Central Oregon that sounded cool: www.experiencethehighlife.tv. He vowed to look at it later when he had more time.

Tony was full of impressions of a college freshman, describing girls he had his eye on. Alex sent a one-liner: *Can't trust a guy in a kilt not to chase after skirts.* He thought his friend would appreciate the joke based on Tony's band uniform for the Ben Lomond High School Scots.

He didn't want to say much else, especially about Jennalee. Best to keep it light, or his temper may show up in the email. He still grappled with anger after getting back from Utah and Tony had been no real help. He didn't know why he avoided answering Pastor Ron's kind note.

Today was Nonna's birthday and the entire Giovanini family would stay for the weekend and dine at the villa for the occasion. Lucio's lovely girls had arrived, already giggling in the kitchen. Gabe would miss the sparkling Gisela, he thought. With a pang, Alex missed his mom and brother.

Nonna, her hair still covered by a netted black hat, swept outside with a tray of croissants. She'd just come from early morning Catholic Mass.

"Have you eaten, *mio caro?*" She moved one of his curls behind his ear.

"*Si*, Nonna, *grazie.*"

She told him in Italian that some old family friends were coming to her birthday celebration.

"Old friends? Let me guess. One of them is the woman you want me to meet."

Her pixie eyes sparkled and he had to smile. "What's her name, Nonna?"

"Firenza Tarentino," said his grandmother with a flourish. "Her family is an old one, with much land. They come from the south as I do."

Alex was good at keeping his emotions from showing, even as he tried to get over Jennalee, so it surprised him when a twinge of excitement welled up at hearing the name. Firenza Tarentino? For Nonna's sake, he'd give this Firenza a chance.

Jennalee faded in and out of his memory like his father did. And by choosing to go on a mission for the LDS Church, wasn't she telling him it was over? So technically, he was free. Maybe he could move on after all.

Nonna gave him a rather wet kiss on the cheek and took off her hat. "*Scusi*, Alessandro," she explained, "I must start the roast."

She set the tray down and rushed into the kitchen to start cooking. Such a large party necessitated the crashing of pots and pans as soon as possible, he thought. Today would be a three-apron day for Nonna, but she'd present a meal so delicious it could be compared to a five-star restaurant. In Italy, tradition held that the person having the birthday must provide the meal for family and friends.

He saw a new email from Gabe and felt guilty sitting in Italian autumn sunlight while his brother was in Utah.

Dear Alex, Ninth grade is okay. Boston Young is in my PE class and told me he couldn't hang out anymore because I'm not LDS. His parents are super mad because Jennalee liked you more than some other guy. I don't want to hang out with him anyway. Oh yeah, Mom went to Starbuck's with a group of people from church. One of them was Jeff Allred. He came by yesterday and played hoops with me, too. Ciao, Gabe P.S. I'm supposed to meet his kids next week. They're a year older than me. Wish you were here.

Wow. A former Mormon, Jeff had come alongside him when he was dating Jennalee. He proved to be a true friend who'd drive by sometimes and join the boys at basketball. Or he'd mow the lawn; whatever they were doing. It might be a good thing, a great thing, his mom and Jeff Allred. And he was way better-looking than old Carl.

This snub at school by Boston made him realize he wasn't able to fix Gabe's problems. But he would pray for his kid brother; public school in Utah took a while to get used to if you weren't in the majority religion. He missed Gabe all the more.

He picked his phone up to text Gabe and there was Jennalee's picture, her blue eyes staring at him, stabbing him in the gut. He'd have to change the picture. His finger hovered over another photo, one of a Maserati. Not yet. He couldn't delete the photo, even if it was painful seeing her face every day.

Honk! Honk! Leaving his laptop open, he rushed through the house and out the tall oak front door as a silver SUV drove into the front circle where a dry fountain graced the ancient villa. He perched himself on the edge of it to greet the kindest aunt and uncle ever, Giuseppe and Adriana. As their four boys piled out of the SUV, Uncle Lucio zoomed up from the fields in a muddy ATV and Nonna trotted outside to shower love and flour on everyone in a chaotic reunion.

Tradition ruled when the seven Giovanini men marched down to the vineyard to see, taste, and feel their grapes. Their land had produced bushels of grapes for hundreds of years. The fruit represented life, a solid foundation on rich soil among decent and honest people. A sense of belonging overwhelmed Alex. He wished he could share his wonderful family heritage with someone, but he didn't think it could ever be Jennalee.

That afternoon, when the outdoor table decorated with linens and flowers was about to be laden with a country feast, a red Mercedes convertible pulled up next to the villa. Lucio, followed by his three daughters, went out to greet the guests.

Alex had taken great care to dress in his best fitted silk shirt and new leather shoes, but hesitated near the door. This is it, he thought. Annoyed with Nonna for setting him up, he smoothed back his unruly hair in front of the hall mirror. He started at his uncle's loud voice.

"My dear, you are *bella*," said Uncle Lucio, helping a striking woman out of the red sports car.

Firenza was tall and blonde, her hair pulled back in a bun on the nape of her neck, so low it touched the back of her dress, a sheath of aqua silk. Balancing sylphlike on black stiletto heels, she glanced around with a shy smile. Was she looking for him?

He agreed with his uncle, she was beautiful. More like stunning. He swallowed and stepped forward to meet her, just as a young man got out of the driver's side and strode with purpose toward Uncle Lucio.

"*Saluto*, Lucio! Remember me? I'm Salvatore."

He extended his hand, but Lucio hugged him, kissing his cheeks, then stepped back, hands atop the young man's shoulders. "You and your sister must be the pride of your father's eyes."

Oh . . . it's her brother, thought Alex. Bolder, he left the shadows and strode out to meet them.

"Come and meet our nephew from America, Alessandro. *Aspetta*, here he is!"

■ ■ ■

At the table, Alex endured his awkwardness among native Italians who'd known each other for years. Nonna, her neck hidden by a mass of pearls, a birthday gift from her sons, gave him a wink as he tried to reassert himself.

He studied Firenza, whose fine features and blond hair probably originated from an ancient Norman bloodline. He knew the Normans held Southern Italy for most of the 11th and 12th centuries and being from northern Europe, they had different features. Her brother had similar traits, though his hair was brown.

Clearly Nonna wanted him to consider dating this attractive young woman, just when he was getting used to not having a girlfriend. His grandmother watched his every move as he posed as the suave business-man Uncle Lucio had coached him to be in front of wealthy Italians. Anything to cover up his intimidation.

Aunt Adriana and the girls placed steaming dishes on the table: roast pork with vegetables, mounded creamy risotto, three different salads, and garlic bread. Uncle Giuseppe's oldest boy, Mateo, poured last year's wine, a prosperous enough vintage to launch their new export business. His cousins, bickering and gesturing, paid no attention to the stilted conversation between him, Firenza, and her brother.

"So . . . where do you live?" Alex finally asked.

She paused. "When we're in Rome, we have a flat near Piazza Navona."

His voice went tight. "Ah, Piazza Navona! I work in Rome twice a week at our shop, the Enoteca Giovanini on Via della Croce. The rest of the time, I'm on the road for our new export business." Too much information; Alex felt himself blush.

"We know Via della Croce well, and Salvatore knows the wine business, too, don't you, *fratello?*"

Salvatore regarded Alex with suspicion. "You are from Chicago? New York?"

"I . . . don't suppose you know where Utah is? Or Oregon?"

Salvatore shook his head but his sister said, "The Great Salt Lake is there, is it not? Salty, like the Dead Sea in the Holy Land of Israel."

Alex nodded, with a sudden picture in his head of sea gulls eating French fries in the grocery store parking lot. "You've got it. I was born in Oregon, but we live in Utah now. My mother teaches college there."

Firenza smiled like the Mona Lisa. "We studied history and geography of the United States at my school in Switzerland." Her flawless English flowed far better than her brother's, who grunted and turned away to speak Italian to cousin Mateo.

After eating Nonna's famous Sicilian *cassata* cake, everyone at the noisy table talked politics, except Lucio who disappeared for several minutes, then rushed back with a tray of wine glasses: two whites and two reds.

He knew what Lucio wanted of him and waved his hands. "No, Zio, I'm full."

"No matter, Alessandro, you must taste to strengthen your skills."

Alex took a deep breath and leaned forward in his chair, his competitive nature challenged. He glanced at Salvatore's serious face. The guy never smiled and his sister . . . well, she was like a statue, mysterious and serene.

Set before Alex on the table, the wines sparkled like jewels. He examined the first glass, relishing the beauty of the liquid.

"I'd say the color is brilliant, medium-bodied, yellow."

He swished the glass as his uncle taught him, releasing nuances of flavor that otherwise wouldn't break through, and took a deep whiff, his nose inside the glass. It never ceased to amaze him how grape juice, when fermented, had the unique ability of all liquids to deliver countless subtle scents and flavors. The privilege of possessing a talent to taste and smell such miraculous beauty was not lost on him.

In the warm Roman sun, he spotted Firenza's soft liquid eyes on him but they seemed detached and remote. What was she thinking? He lifted the glass, understanding that for him, some beauty held hidden dangers.

"Well, Uncle, definitely grapefruit, with melon overtones." He took another sniff. "I also detect a scent of dried hay."

His uncle wore no expression, but Alex suspected he was on the right track, and sipped from the glass. Salvatore's face was unreadable under the umbrellas above the table.

"It's slightly oaky from the barrel; balanced on acidity and fruit. Tannin's firm. Am I right to assume this wine is made from the Trebbiano grape?"

Not a muscle in Lucio's face moved, but his eyes sparkled. Alex hesitated, and then slurped the wine, savoring the strong taste. "I maintain this wine is Trebbiano, from L'Abruzzo."

Cousin Mateo nodded with an easy smile, but Uncle Lucio stared hard at Alex. "Hmm, I see your American fast food has not yet ruined your palate. Which vineyard?"

"Putifaro?" He knew he shouldn't guess.

"No, my son, the rival vineyard, the famous Bonavita."

Alex called his uncle's bluff. "Bonavita? The name of our kitchen coffeemaker?" Everyone laughed, even Salvatore, while Firenza maintained that Mona Lisa smile.

"No, Uncle, it belongs to Putifaro's real rival, Valentini."

Lucio clapped his hands, delighted. "*Si, bravissimo*, now for the others."

Sliding into a chair beside Firenza, Nonna's approval was all over her face. Her wrinkled maternal hand rested on Firenza's perfectly manicured one.

After Alex identified each wine correctly, everyone gave a happy salutatory raise of glasses to Nonna's birthday, her health, and fine cooking as well as a productive harvest. The next hour of conversation loosened up, becoming jovial. Alex gained respect for Salvatore's knowledge of wines, while Firenza joined the women in a tour of the villa's new gardens.

When it was time for the Giovaninis to escort their guests back to the car, Firenza surprised Alex with a light kiss on the cheek, saying she enjoyed the relaxed afternoon meal in the garden, and hoped she'd see him again in the city. It was only a peck, but as they waved goodbye, he felt Nonna's eyes on him.

A petite four foot ten, her back curving with age, his little grandmother approached and took his arm. They walked together down the cypress lined road, the red convertible in the dusty distance in front of them. At last she spoke. "How you like my *bella* Firenza?"

"I do, Nonna, but I'm not sure I'm ready to . . ."

"She wants to see you in Rome. You must see her there."

He switched to Italian. "I probably will, only I make no promises, Nonna."

"Alessandro," she answered, her voice soft. "I only want the best for you. I see you pining away for a girl who never answers you, so here is a pretty girl who likes you. Why don't you take her to lunch when you're in Rome?"

"Nonna, I'm so . . . out of my element."

"What do you mean?"

"These are rich people. When she finds out the truth about who I am, she'll run the other way."

"You are good enough. You're a Giovanini."

They strolled back to the villa arm in arm where they could see the rest of the family spreading out to play in the twilight: taking rides on the ATV, kicking a soccer ball, splashing in the pool and setting up chess-boards. Gabe would've loved this.

From a window, an upstairs speaker played the opera "The Barber of Seville," with his favorite, 'Figaro' aria, sung by Luciano Pavarotti. This was a family favorite, a CD he'd heard many times at his grandmother's house.

"Figaro here, Figaro there, Figaro up, Figaro down . . ." Alex sang in English in his operatic voice, making Nonna laugh. If only his life would be as lucky as Figaro's.

At the moon's rising, Giuseppe's family took over the entire upstairs bedrooms, so Alex had to share his room with the two oldest boys, Mateo and Daniele. Seeing them was like seeing his reflection in the mirror. Most people thought them brothers with their luxuriant hair, but when they spoke, his Italian was flecked with an American accent. He couldn't pass for a native-born Italian and he didn't want to. After all, his dad was second generation American and he was proud of that fact.

Mateo was as kind as his father, easy-going and cool-headed. Coming in from the bathroom, he put his toothbrush back in his bag and asked, "So how do you like Firenza Tarentino, Alessandro?"

"She's . . . let's face it, I mean, wow, she's good-looking. You've known her a long time, haven't you?"

"All my life, but she's way older than me."

"She's only a year older than me," said Alex, "which might work . . ."

Daniele spoke up. "He means because of the age difference, we don't know her very well, Alessandro. When we were small, she used to try to play games with us, like chess. But her brother ignored us. I wish your brother was here with us. I see him only twice this summer; we have so much fun at the beach, *fantastico*." Daniele was a livewire of a teenager who loved pranks so Alex imagined Gabe *did* have fun with him.

"He wished he could stay, believe me, he wanted to be here for Nonna's birthday."

"Zio Lucio said you went back to America to . . ." Daniele stumbled on his words. "Eh . . . he said you must see about the *cavoli riscaldati*."

"Did you just say 'reheated cabbage'?" Alex was sure he misunderstood.

Mateo looked stern. "Daniele shouldn't have brought it up. It is untranslatable in English. It means you try to save a dead love affair, which is messy and not so good, like . . ."

"I get it, like reheated cabbage." It hit him hard and annoyed him. "It's not exactly like that. Uncle Lucio wonders why I didn't bring my girlfriend back. You guys wouldn't believe how complicated it is." Maybe they were right and it was like a bowl of stringy cabbage after all.

Mateo scolded Daniele in rapid Italian. Alex couldn't catch much of it and held his hand up.

"Stop, Mateo, I'm okay about it. In fact, it's a pretty descriptive term of my life. Now I get to ask you two a question. What do you guys *really* think of Firenza?"

Daniele only gave a low whistle. "She's rich, she's *bella*. What's to think about?" He switched off the light.

They all climbed into bed under blue matelassé covers that the moonlight made into silver. Mateo took his time answering. "She is very beautiful, but also very cold."

Daniele, more animated, explained further. "A perfect statue made of ice, never breaking. It's strange to me. I think it's the opposite of being Italian. It's like she's from somewhere else."

Taken aback by their answers, Alex said, "Icy or not, she strikes me as just being shy."

Mateo switched to Italian. "She's not shy. Just the opposite, she's self-confident. Firenza Tarentino has always been this way, Alessandro. No emotion. Some people think it's because she had to go to school in Switzerland her whole life."

"She told me. Lots of rich people send their kids away, but she had a good education there. Speaks English like a pro."

Mateo expounded. "They are very rich. The Tarentinos are like royalty in Venetia where we live. You should see their estate up there, but I hear their southern one is even larger."

"It must be *molto bene* with lots of land," added Daniele. Even in the dark, Alex could tell he stretched his hands out wide.

"It's a sad story," Mateo began, "their mother was much younger than their father. He's old enough to be their grandfather." The rustling of covers told Alex that Mateo must've sat up in bed.

"What happened to her?"

"Alessandro, it was terrible. Their mother was killed in a car accident the day before Firenza's baptism when she was eight days old and Salvatore was only two. Their father never remarried."

"How does Nonna know the family?"

Mateo took a deep breath. "Leo Tarentino is the same age as Nonna. They grew up together. He knew her before she married Papa." Alex sensed rather than saw Mateo bow his head and make a sign of the cross, touching head, chest, and shoulders with outstretched fingers. "God rest Papa's soul. Some say she broke Leo's heart when she married Papa."

"I wonder if Nonna ever loved him. I mean, there's some story here no one's telling us."

"We've tried to find out more, but Nonna insists they're only old friends."

"Could be *he* still loves her." Was it a case of hope deferred? There was more to this tale and he'd try to find out. But not now, he thought, yawning. "Maybe Firenza's cold because her mom died when she was a baby."

"Possibly, Alessandro. So she's not as cold as she is sad, no?" Mateo said from his pillow, also yawning. "*Buona notte, cugino.*"

That's it, she's sad, he thought. Whether Nonna wanted a connection between their families or for him to live in Italy the rest of his life, he wasn't sure, but clearly she thought he'd be happy with Firenza Tarentino, even if she was a year older. He had to admit her perfect beauty fit into his new world of sharp shoes, silk ties and designer sunglasses, but she was a far cry from the simple bumming-around-in-a-truck Alex from Utah.

Remembering how Jennalee kicked her shoes off to dance at the prom brought a pained furrow to his forehead. She'd loved riding around in the old truck. It was a mess alright, a regular *cavoli riscaldati*, but he held on to a thin thread of hope that somehow he'd not been wrong about God's plan for them to be together. He drifted to sleep, with a pang of guilt that he hadn't once looked at the online church his mom had told him about. Something about the high life . . .

6

OUTSIDE THE CAMP

The Salt Lake City airport welcomed him when Brent Young arrived home from his mission in Argentina. It was the exact day his sister Jennalee waited in a different terminal of the airport to leave for her mission. Hugging his parents, he couldn't imagine the roller coaster they endured, so he held back revealing to them where he stood with the Church until after his welcome party. He knew they would not be happy.

When all the guests had left, he went to his father's den to announce he no longer believed the Church was true. He tried not to see their pale faces as he told them. "I don't believe in the Book of Mormon anymore. I believe in the real Jesus Christ and His Cross and I've given my life to Him. I love you both very much, but I can't be in the Church anymore." Head up, he walked out and went upstairs to his bedroom, leaving his parents in sputtering shock.

In his room, Brent paced the carpet. The Church talked far more about its founder, Joseph Smith, than about Jesus. And the Jesus of the LDS Church was not the one he now had a relationship with. That LDS Savior constantly admonished him to be an exact clone of Himself resulting in a torrent of guilt and unworthiness. How could he have known that his life would be completely changed by the Jesus of the Bible?

Until his mission in Argentina, Brent never had a chance to think in a more logical way about his faith. In high school seminary, he'd been told that 'when LDS leaders speak, the thinking's been done' and the statement hadn't sat well with him. Members weren't supposed to ask *why* they believed. And you weren't supposed to ever doubt.

Many LDS believers testified of a 'burning in the bosom' feeling when seeking if the LDS Scriptures were true, but he'd never experienced that burning. At first he blamed his sinfulness, but soon he wondered whether he should trust feelings when it came to finding truth.

When he read the New Testament, it said that salvation came through Jesus alone. Not a church. Not a prophet. Not a temple ordinance. The excruciating pain of realizing his childhood religion wouldn't stand up to his adult scrutiny caused anger and confusion at first. Then he met Rachel, the first born-again believer he'd ever talked to.

Now he searched his suitcase for the scrap of paper she'd given him, wanting to let her know he was back in the States. Brent opened his desktop and typed a few lines to Rachel. She could be counted on to pray for him, he knew.

He saw a note from Jennalee. How could she know what misery transpired that evening at the affluent house at the foot of the Wasatch Mountains? And he'd caused it.

> *Welcome home, Brent! I'm sad I can't see you, but excited to get to Italy. I may as well tell you I fell absolutely in love with a guy named Alex Campanaro last year. And he's a born-again Christian. Don't tell Mom and Dad. They had no idea how serious we were and I still don't know what to tell them. I guess it doesn't matter now because I have no contact with Alex. I feel lost without him. Write me soon. I love you, dear brother and hope your homecoming is blessed. Jennalee*

So he was not alone. If his sister had fallen for an evangelical Christian, stakes were higher than ever for his staunch LDS parents. They would make sure their four youngest sons wouldn't fall away from the Church like him and his sister.

He guessed his dad, in his anger, had already decided what to do with him; how to punish him. Dad must not find out about Jennalee, even if she doubted the faith a tiny bit. He suspected Alex had the same effect on her that Rachel had on him. Brent wished he could see Jennalee; he knew he could open up to her about his whole spiritual journey.

If he'd known how serious she was with Alex, he wouldn't have urged her to go on a mission. Their parents probably thought she'd left her affections for a non-Mormon behind by choosing a mission so she was not under suspicion, although they may have guessed she was dodging marriage to a guy she didn't love.

He wanted to know how close she was to accepting Alex's faith. She hadn't revealed her own feelings. Brent wrote back in a hurry, knowing it would take a full week for her to receive it.

> Hi Jennalee, what news! Is Alex Campanaro here in Kaysville? Maybe I could help you find him. First, I have to pick up my companion, Ammon, next week. He's coming home from his mission in Argentina and his parents can't meet him at the airport. It's a long story, but I have to help him out by taking him to Price, and I can't stay here at home anyway. My life changed and I never saw it coming. I don't want to say much until the smoke clears with Mom and Dad. You always give me good advice when it came to girls, so I have to tell you I think I met THE girl in Argentina. No matter what you hear about me, I love all my family. Brent
> PS Now I'm sorry I told you to go on a mission.

He closed his eyes and pressed SEND. It would be better to tell her about his change in faith later, when he was out of the house; he didn't want his parents to think he'd unduly influenced her in any way. Besides, she was probably as excited as he'd been after the MTC experience . . . until some irreconcilable realities about his faith and his life hit him square in the face.

Rachel, the evangelical Christian girl he met while she volunteered at an orphanage in Buenos Aires, was his main encourager. The first day he saw her, Brent was struck by her petite figure. She wore a T-shirt with a bold cross on it, her oval face framed in French braids of dark brown hair. He remembered how she shone with patience and compassion throughout the torturous questions he peppered at her for three months. He cringed when he thought about it.

Those conversations flowed as they worked side by side at an orphanage near the slums. He and Ammon tried to sway Rachel and her friend Alison into Mormonism, breaking some rules as they went, but on his part, it fast became a half-hearted effort. Jesus' love emanated from those girls; clearer and brighter than the airbrushed paintings in the temple. Missionary methods of persuasion and role-playing practiced at the MTC broke down.

"I'm not talking about religion," she told him one day as they scrubbed the dreary walls of the orphanage. Ammon was within earshot, allowing Brent to discuss the LDS points they'd been taught to share.

"Of course that's what we're talking about," said Ammon, who blushed every time either girl came near him.

"All we have to do is know Jesus is God," Rachel said.

He remembered how his neck stiffened. "Miss Christenson, that's not the only point. As an LDS member, I have a living Prophet to directly tell me what God is saying, and every ordinance to ensure Celestial Heaven if I obey. I bear testimony of this truth." Ammon regarded him with awe.

"Jesus *is* salvation because he is God," Rachel replied. "We need no other."

"We both know there's more to it; there are commandments to obey."

"Let me tell you what an Argentinean evangelist named Luis Palau said on the radio. He said, 'Want to know why I hate religion and love Jesus? Because religion says *do*, Jesus says *done*. Religion says *slave*, Jesus says *free*.'"

Seeing her pretty face lit up by an inner glow when she said this, he felt like an animal who'd wandered on the road at night and was blinded by headlights.

"All you need to do is tell Jesus you want this kind of relationship, Elder Young. Ask him your questions. He loves you." Unruffled, she passed by him to rummage for something in her backpack and he was so close he could see the top of her hair spiraled in a braid.

She held out an iPod and speaker. "You said you liked the songs we played yesterday. Want to borrow some music?"

This was worship music like he'd never heard before. Compared to the stiff hymns he was used to, this music was fresh. It filled him with hope.

"I can't," he stammered.

Ammon spoke up to help him. "We can only listen to or read Church-approved materials."

Rachel plugged it in with the small speaker. "Well, Alison and I want to hear the new 'Mercy Me' song if you guys don't mind." Her friend nodded and Brent tensed, sensing Ammon's disapproval, but thirsty to hear it himself.

Arguments eventually died down because the girls became genuine friends. One day he and Ammon told them about the telephone game; where children sit in a row and by whispering in the ear of the person next to them, communicate a phrase. As the saying is passed down the line by so many people, it is changed into something totally different than the original.

"I remember that game," Alison said, "you say you played it in Sunday school?"

"Same thing only we call it Primary," answered Ammon, "and it was to prove a point."

Brent said, "The point was the Bible can't be trusted because of translation mistakes over the centuries."

Ammon was elated, like they were getting somewhere with their doctrines. "We believe the Bible was controlled by a corrupt church so it's not trustworthy."

A stunned silence in the room forced him to see that the girls were distressed. "It makes me sad that anybody would tell little kids this story and apply it to the Bible. Don't you think God would make sure his Word survived in all of its truth?" said Rachel.

"No, ma'am. It's why we needed the Book of Mormon," Ammon answered her.

Rachel's face fell and Alison spoke for her. "Didn't they teach you about how the ancient manuscripts were meticulously copied by scribes onto scrolls? Every little dot?"

"Like the Dead Sea Scrolls?" Brent asked. "They were on display in Salt Lake City, I saw them."

"Then you also saw how they confirm the accuracy of our present Bible and what mainline Christians believe," said Alison.

Brent saw Rachel's sad face and inside, a tidal wave knocked him into the sand. He had to admit he didn't know much of the Old Testament, or the New. He only knew plucked out passages missionaries used to convince others to convert. He didn't know any of it like these two born-again girls did.

He remembered some of his LDS friends mocking and ridiculing born-again Christians, and he'd joined in. But at that time, they'd never met one, much less talked to them. Now he had, and what could he say about these attractive young women who'd swept away his comfort zone forever?

Rachel's quiet voice resonated. "Something huge is missing in your lives."

Brent saw her intense eyes burning with . . . what was it? He desperately wanted to know what she thought was missing, but he made a dogged effort to defend Mormonism one more time. "We have everything we need; the sacred temple ordinances, the Book of Mormon, and a living prophet to tell us exactly what God says. What could we be missing?"

Rachel softened. "Spiritual eyes and ears to understand." She took a slow breath and swiped away perspiration from her forehead. "But you can ask Jesus and he will give them to you."

In that instant, Brent remembered feeling like he was swimming against a strong current, about to be swept away. He'd always been competitive; wanting others to see him as a Mormon of Mormons, perfect in all he did. So when the petite girl made him feel weak, he flailed in anger against the unfamiliar tide of doubt.

He recalled times in his childhood when he felt glimmers of pure joy. One summer evening, alone in the house, he'd watched a Billy Graham biography on TV. How different the Southern preacher sounded than the speakers at General Conference. He hadn't completely understood the man's message, but a wave of joy swept over him as he sat on the couch watching. Rachel was right, there was something missing and it had to do with joy.

Spiritual eyes and ears to understand. That was what she'd said, and later, that's what he asked for, alone at night, with Ammon sleeping in the cot beside him. And slowly, in little whispers, Brent saw and heard things he'd never understood or imagined. Leafing through his fat Quad of LDS scriptures, he came upon obscure passages in the New Testament that repeated inside his brain, catapulting him into a state of joy. There were no words for a high like that.

Brent remembered Rachel's face, clear and peaceful. Her faith affected him in a way difficult to forget, so . . . weeks before he left Argentina, he woke up on a drizzly August day, and knew if he were honest he could no longer be a Latter-day Saint. For him, it had become all about the Jesus of the Cross.

■ ■ ■

Memories melted away when he heard shouting downstairs. Brent tiptoed down the long staircase and sat on the last stair, elbows on his knees, so he could hear what was being said in the den. Hours ago, he'd made his announcement of unbelief in that very room. He heard his mom crying.

"Give him some time, Rulon, he's only been back forty-eight hours. Lots of missionaries have a hard time adjusting when they come back to America."

"I don't know, Marge, but I know one thing, he's different than the boy we sent on a mission, and not in a good way. It's a bad omen, first Jennalee with her fixation on that Baptist or whatever, and now this blatant unbelief with Brent. I never thought he would do this . . . to us."

To hear his father's voice break was almost more than Brent could bear. He felt like running into the room and hugging them, telling them it would be okay, but he knew it wouldn't be; it would never be okay again. He *was* different inside and nothing they could say or do would ever change him back to the twenty year-old they'd said goodbye to two years ago.

"It's breaking my heart, too," said his mother. "But we have to resolve our four youngest won't go the way of the world, they will stay forever in Zion."

"You're absolutely right. Who would've thought Brent would go astray? It should have been the opposite." Brent could hear confusion and anger in his father's voice.

"Now, Rul, he's only said these things to us, and we can hide it. He'll get an honorable discharge because he wasn't in trouble the whole two years."

"I can make sure of it; I know who to call about this . . ."

Rather than hear more, Brent slipped out the front door. With sadness under an autumn moon, he walked for hours in the old neighborhood, his stomach sick in grief for his dying childhood faith and for the loss of his family and friends.

He and all other LDS children had been given a narrative, and children cannot help what they are taught. If he wasn't allowed to question or doubt or research things as an adult, then his faith wasn't his own.

Much as his parents hoped for an honorable discharge, the bishop of the Church would require him to make a public testimony, which he wondered if he could do in honesty. Fear set in, but he resolved to tell the truth he'd found.

As he stood in front of the darkened brick building that'd been his ward chapel since he'd been born, he knew he should leave home and the discomfort of being outside the camp. But he had to love them, really love them through it all. It felt strange to pray using words he would use to a human friend, but as he walked, a prayer just slipped out.

"Jesus, I didn't know you but you stooped down and lit a fire in me no one can quench. When I asked, you gave me eyes to see and ears to hear. My people don't have them yet, they don't understand, so be with me when

I go to the bishop and protect me from the anger of my parents, who I know you love. Jesus, I trust in you and your mercy."

A moonlit peace carried away the enormous weight of fear and guilt, replacing it with an unfamiliar feeling of freedom here on the streets of his childhood. As he wandered through the darkness of his former world, his steps became more certain. He resolved to tell everyone who would listen what changed him in Argentina because it was the greatest treasure of his life.

7

TEMPTATION

Alex almost forgot an important meeting at ten the next morning with *Signore* Putifaro, a vineyard owner and oenophile who liked to play at mentoring him when it came to wine tasting. Dressed in his custom gray suit, he climbed into the Maserati to drive to the Putifaro villa in the northern outskirts of Rome. It would be hard to concentrate on business today with his curiosity about the new woman in his life, Firenza.

Largo Putifaro was a well-known client around Rome and the Abruzzo region, as large as his name in wealth and well-fed girth. The man's huge ego bothered Alex; his uncle, not so much.

"Of course, his pride is enormous," Uncle Lucio told him, "and he drinks too much. If you humor him, all the better. Be agreeable, my son, and you'll get the contract. Americans will buy his wine."

"Why did Largo marry someone twenty years younger? He's at least sixty."

"He's been through several wives, and now he fancies himself young again. Perhaps she is the last wife."

The Putifaros owned a massive vineyard in Abruzzo as well as the Roman villa where Alex was to meet them. He guessed Caprice would be there; she always was when he had a meeting with her husband. When

Alex first encountered her at an evening wine-tasting party, he noticed she had an eye for young, athletic men but her husband was oblivious to this fact.

Alex was unsure of Caprice's intentions and her presence gave him a feeling of dread. Still, he had a job to do, and the Abruzzo wine produced by their vineyard soared high on Uncle Lucio's list.

So Alex put the errant wife's behavior in the back of his mind when he drove up and parked in the round driveway surfaced with white crushed rock. With false confidence he struck the knocker on the imposing front door. Almost immediately, the hinges moved and there she was, in a low-cut blouse and piled-on makeup.

She'd look better without all that, thought Alex, irritated. An amazing amount of flirtatious energy flowed from her mouth.

"Ah, it is you, Alessandro. I bring you to my husband in the barrel vault in the cellar. You are here to taste wines, no?"

"I'll wait for him here, *Signora*," he said. "Does he have his cell phone with him? I can text him." He got his phone out and Caprice saw Jennalee's picture on his background.

"Your girlfriend?" She smirked.

"Um . . . yes." Alex gulped. At least she used to be.

In a snap second, Caprice took his phone, and tossed it on a foyer table. "Leave her here," she said, taking his arm and pulling him out the door in the direction of the wine cellar and across the courtyard. "I take you to my husband."

"*Signora*, with all respect, your husband and I habitually meet in the house. Did he forget I was coming? He prepares me wines to taste in his office."

"He forgets much but he will want to see you. Come with me."

Alex had no choice but to keep up with her as she gripped his arm and led him towards an outbuilding, her high heels crunching the tiny pieces of rock. Nearby, a skinny boy whose hair stuck straight up on his head darted into the shadows.

"Who's that?" he asked her.

"My brother's son; he's no good but my husband keeps him around." She cursed the boy with loud obscenities while he watched them from behind a corner. Grabbing Alex's arm all the tighter, she escorted him to a stone stairwell leading into darkness. Later he remembered the echo when, standing on the edge of the top stair, he asked, "Are you sure he's down here, *Signora?*"

"You do not believe me? Today he is below ground in his vault," she breathed, her red lipstick shining in the dim light, "call me Caprice, not *Signora*, Alessandro."

His name trilled off her tongue. She led the way, her hips in a thin pencil skirt swaying unnaturally as she descended into the darkness. His uneasiness increased and with it a heady feeling as if he were being led to the gallows.

Caprice was pretty, her figure curvy, and she clearly liked him. He took a deep breath of the damp air; it did nothing to clear his head, instead intoxicating him with perfume mixed with ancient stone and Roman brick. A kind of adrenaline rush coursed through his veins.

They reached a hallway lined with casks of wine, eerily lit with fluorescent light. The woman pivoted like a cat, cornering him near a barrel, bringing her body way closer to him than he liked. He tried to retain his composure.

"Today, I am the one who set out wine for you, Alessandro." She extended a manicured hand in the beckoning gesture of certain women everywhere. He'd seen it in movies, but wasn't it somewhere in the book of Proverbs? His mother had raised him on it, and all of sudden, he recognized this whole scene.

"Where is your husband?" Alex asked, his voice resounding through the damp vault. He tried to put arm's length between them. "*Signore* Putifaro isn't here, is he? You led me down here for nothing."

"For nothing, Alessandro? I know your uncle, I know him well. If you refuse, Lucio will be disappointed in you. See, the wine is there, on the table."

A glass of white wine sparkled on an oak barrel with a single rose arranged on a white napkin near it.

"*Signora*, you say you know my uncle. Lucio wouldn't want . . ."

"Alessandro, why so nervous, don't you trust me? You thinking too much about your little blonde?" Her chin jutted high; her eyes formed slits in the dim light.

"SIGNORE PUTIFARO!" As Alex shouted into the dark, Caprice threw herself, pushing him into one of the enormous barrels stretching down the long hallway of the vault. A spigot hurt his shoulder where she pressed as she tried to kiss him. Clawing with fanglike fingers, she tore at his shirt collar, then gripped his head to hers with spider hands.

"If you will not taste the wine, you will taste my lips," she purred, planting her full red mouth on his.

Shock overcame him for a second, but he found himself liking her closeness. A half-second later repulsion and shame overtook him, almost making him sick. He brushed her off, wanting to spit the syrupy taste of lipstick out of his mouth. "No, this is wrong. You're married, *Signora. . ."*

"Largo is far down the tunnel, he will not know, Alessandro," she purred.

With both hands around her waist, Alex picked her up off her feet and sat her down with a crash on the table. He heard the shoulder seams of his suit coat ripping as the wine glass skittered over the tiles, shattering, spilling amber liquid across the floor.

The fury in her eyes shone with pure hatred. Insulted by his rejection, she jeered, "You are no man but a boy. You will pay for this." She spat at him, barely missing his face, then jumped off the cask like a cat, lowering her blouse so she appeared violated. Speeding down the vault, high heels clicking on the tile floor, she screamed, "Largo! Largo! Look what he do to me!" Her rotund husband stumbled into the main hallway from another area, glass in hand.

Alex spun around to escape. His feet pounded up the stairs as he fled. Shouts and curses echoed behind him. Would the old man believe her? From what he knew of him, Largo Putifaro's pride wouldn't allow him to admit his wife tried to seduce other men. There goes this contract, he thought. His uncle would chide him for the loss, so maybe Caprice was right, he would pay for this.

He swung into the Maserati, started the engine and roared out of the driveway, white rock chips flying. Alex felt tainted, disgusted by both her and himself. He should never have followed her, he knew that now.

Inching his arms out of his perfume laden torn jacket, he threw it on the floor and turned up his music, hoping the pop station on the radio would put miles between him and the incident. Maybe there wouldn't be a backlash. Stopping at a wide spot in the road, he reached for his cell to call Uncle Lucio. It wasn't in his pocket; it was on the Putifaro's table.

8

A SAINT ARRIVES IN THE ETERNAL CITY

"Talk about culture shock," said Terrilyn McKay, Jennalee's new missionary companion, as soon as they met up in Italy. In contrast, Jennalee found the new country exciting, even invigorating, and she kept silent at the girl's complaints.

"Oh my heck, I can't believe the way they do things here. The Rome airport was a chaotic mess; they talk so fast and yell at each other. American airports are more organized." Terrilyn wrinkled her nose. "Is that garlic I smell?"

"The airport was chaotic because of a delay in London. It's not Italy's fault several international flights came in at the same time." Jennalee defended the place although the noise and chaos surprised her, too.

Terrilyn McKay's narrow face pinched into a frown. "Not to mention the enormous amount of Euros we were forced to pay the taxi to take us to our crummy rented room." She practically hyperventilated. "Another obnoxious scooter. It's crazy here."

Jennalee waited for the noise of the motorbike to dissipate. "Terrilyn . . ." Her companion gave her a stern stare. "I mean Sister McKay . . . if we'd taken the bus like we were supposed to, we wouldn't be out all the money for the taxi."

"The bus was packed; I didn't want to stand, did you?"

"We have to get used to this place, Sister McKay; we're going to be here a long time."

"You're scratching your garments again, Sister Young. It's annoying."

"Sorry," said Jennalee, "I think I'm allergic to the fabric. I got the wrong kind."

How will I wear them the rest of my life? The LDS under-garments bestowed to her during the endowment ceremony at the Kaysville temple were a daily reminder of the promises and covenants she'd made to God in the temple. Definitely.

"Are you used to yours yet?"

"Of course. C'mon, you've been wearing them for months now. What's wrong with you? Keep sweet."

Jennalee felt guilty but didn't answer. As a child, she often saw her mother fanning herself in the summer because the extra layer of clothing was just plain hot. She knew she'd have to suffer through and not complain, like her mother did.

Terrilyn looked thoughtful. "Have you ever been out of Utah?"

"No." Jennalee wished she could've said the opposite. Still tired from jet lag, the two went out in the late afternoon on the day of their arrival to get some food.

"Me neither, only I've been to the Salt Lake airport often enough and it's clean and nice and organized. At least it's sane at home in Utah."

"Sane? Have you ever driven south on the freeway to Provo on a Friday about this time? You call that sane?"

"We don't have much traffic in Logan, where I'm from."

For Jennalee, walking in the Eternal City of Rome after landing hours ago was a thrill, full of combined exotic sounds. The tinkling of silverware from open windows, honking car horns and scooters, and cawing of crows in the umbrella pines convinced her Italy held adventure for her. Hearing the beauty of the Italian language itself, sometimes spoken, sometimes sung, was a joy.

"Tomorrow is our preparation day so we can check our email," said Terrilyn. "The other days we stick to our schedule: get ready, eat breakfast, and do our personal studies. Then we do our companion studies, say our testimonies, and we'll be out at 9:30, like at the MTC."

"I'll be glad to have email time. My brother Brent came back from his mission the day I left, so between his and mine, I won't see him for three and a half years. I'm expecting to hear from him." She wasn't about to tell Terrilyn about the hoped-for news from Alex.

"I have no brothers, only sisters. I'm the oldest. What's your brother like?" Jennalee could see her companion's interest when she heard Brent was a returned missionary. It made him primary marriage material to every LDS girl.

"Brent and I can talk about anything. And he always protected me at school from anyone teasing me."

Terrilyn cocked her head. "I assume he's in college?"

"He went to BYU to study pre-law. My brother's smart. He'll probably go back next semester."

"Well? Does he have a girlfriend or fiancé?"

"He did mention someone in his last letter but I'm not sure she's actually his girlfriend." She was used to questions about her brother from every friend she had.

They purchased Panini sandwiches from a corner café, then went back to their room in a strategic building near the Spanish Steps, located to talk to as many people as they could, including tourists. They both knew Rome was dead center to Roman Catholicism and skeptics at the MTC warned them that finding converts on their assignment would be rough. They unpacked more and the evening blurred into night as she drifted to sleep, still listening to late dinner sounds outside the open window. It *was* garlic, that strong aroma in the air. . .

■ ■ ■

When the foreign street sounds woke her at six, Jennalee was ready to explore, but her companion dragged her feet. "We need food," she told Terrilyn, "we don't even have anything for breakfast."

"We have protein bars. Hey, yesterday you said you didn't know whether your brother had a girlfriend or not," Terrilyn said, as she picked up her curling iron. "You'll tell him about *me*, won't you?"

Jennalee frowned. She would tell Brent about Sister McKay alright, but the girl didn't have a clue *what* she would tell him.

As Terrilyn asked this bossy question, a burning smell pervaded the little room where they had only a microwave and a small fridge.

"Oh no! My curling iron! I know I brought the right adaptor. I know I did!" The bottom of a wispy curl fell to the floor, singed off.

Jennalee stifled a smile. "We'll have to find another curling iron, if we can find a store. Internet café first, though." Email was priority.

"We need the Italian equivalent of Wal-Mart, and where would that be around here? Those are out in the suburbs." Terrilyn picked up the burned curl and threw it away with a long sigh.

"Next week we're supposed to go to a Church member's house for dinner. It's out in the suburbs near the Appian Way."

"How are we going to get there?" Terrilyn tied her hair in a ponytail.

"We'll catch a bus." Little did Terrilyn know Jennalee had studied every guidebook to Rome she could in the last two weeks. Her sole mission was to find Alex in Italy.

She considered the sour face of the companion who would be by her side for the next eighteen months unless the higher-ups changed things. Brent had hoped she'd get as nice a companion as he got, but Terrilyn was going to take patience. Lots of it.

They went through the MTC morning drill, then went out. Jennalee found herself stopping in her tracks every time she saw a guy with wild curly hair. She had to make sure it wasn't Alex.

"Sister Young, you're awfully distracted by the men here," Terrilyn stated. "You need to forget about them. They're probably all Catholic."

"Probably," she answered, "so you're right." Smiling inside, she could only think about the one guy she wanted to find. Why had she thought it would be easy?

Rome's climate was affected by the sea and cool morning overcast burned off by noon, far different than the consistent dryness of the Rocky

Mountains where she was from. As the day grew hot, they found the internet café. "I'm already homesick," said Terrilyn, "I wish I was anywhere but here."

"For me, it's not homesickness as much as hearing from my brother and home."

No mail from Alex. Her parents sent a loving note with news about the people of their ward chapel, and her brother Boston wrote about school. Then she saw a message from Brent.

> *Hi, Sis,*
>
> *I'm going to Price where Ammon lives in a few days. I have to stick around to get my RM discharge. I don't know what Mom and Dad have told you, but I have more to tell you about where I'm at. We've been apart so long; I wish I could talk to you face to face. Mom and Dad gave me a new smart phone, so I'll watch for your emails on it. Love, Brent*

What an unsatisfying letter. Why wasn't he mentioning going back to BYU? Something was up with Brent and her parents. Pursing her lips, she wrote back.

> *Hi, Brent.*
>
> *What do you have to tell me? I wish you could tell me face to face, too. I love Italy, but my companion is a whiner. Alex is not in Kaysville, he's here in Italy. I hope to find him somehow. Love, Jennalee*

With his smart phone, he should've answered. She waited for him to answer as she dealt with the other mail, but her thirty minutes ended, and nothing.

"You're deep in thought," her companion said, tapping her shoulder, "you didn't hear me say our time's up."

"My brother sent me a strange email. Something's going on, that's all. Probably nothing to worry about." She couldn't help slipping in, "And I didn't hear from . . . a close friend."

Sister McKay's eyebrows rose, but she didn't say anything.

■ ■ ■

That evening, the young women were supposed to meet with two male counterparts for a dinner meeting. Before they left their room, Terrilyn primped until the pungent smell of hair spray overpowered any delicious cooking smells from the family kitchens around their apartment building.

"C'mon, we'll be late," said Jennalee.

"It's just across the Piazza del Popolo in the restaurant we scouted out today." Terrilyn slammed down her curling iron. "I hate this Italian thing, it doesn't work like mine."

Jennalee rolled her eyes. "At least it doesn't burn your hair. I'm ready. You coming?"

Her companion annoyed her many times but the worst thing was that Terrilyn proved to be perpetually slow. When they entered the restaurant agreed upon, there were already two white-shirted, dark-suited elders sitting inside. "Told you we'd be late," she whispered to Terrilyn, who paid no attention as she blinked at the men.

Terrilyn smoothed her skirt. "I'll take the one on the left. Oh my heck, he's cute."

Exasperated, Jennalee peeked at the two clean-cut missionaries and agreed one guy *was* good-looking, with close-cropped dark hair and a muscular physique. For a second, she was tempted to do a little harmless flirting, but she squelched it. Just because she hadn't heard from Alex in months, didn't mean she could stray from him.

"You can have them both," she told her companion.

Terrilyn, giggling, sat close to dark-haired Elder Perry, who inched his chair back a bit at her brazen attitude. Jennalee sat next to the other missionary. After some chitchat, they got down to business.

"So tomorrow you're going out to the New Appian Way to Sister Agosta's house for dinner?" said the elder, whose nametag said Almandson. "She's a superb cook, only watch out for her son. He'll pinch you." The two men laughed.

"Coarse joking, Elders," said Terrilyn, "it's such an old cliché that men pinch women in these Latin countries."

"You haven't been here long, have you?" the Elder replied.

"Two days," said Jennalee, "so I guess we haven't."

"How do you li . . . like . . . Italy, Sister Young?" asked Elder Perry. Poor guy, she thought, he's so handsome, but stutters.

"So far I love it. This morning I smelled marinara sauce cooking. They simmer it all day. I even heard our next door neighbor singing opera. You don't get opera much in Utah unless you go to the University. Where are you from, Elder?"

Elder Perry deferred with a nod to the obvious leader of the pair, the louder Elder Almandson. In England he'd be called ginger-haired, she thought. "I'm from Sandy, and Elder Perry's from Morgan. Not much opera in Morgan, is there?" He laughed with disdain. "Personally, I don't like the smells here."

His attitude angered her. How could a man with such a superior attitude appreciate this unique country? The four studied each other. All were from Utah, sent to ground zero of Roman Catholicism. The Prophet must have deemed it necessary to send the most confident, Utah-born young people to spread Joseph Smith's teachings in such a tough mission field. She should've been proud, but knew their efforts to gain converts would result in rejection. She couldn't help but think that's how poor Elder Perry acquired a stutter.

"How long have you been in Rome?" Terrilyn asked.

"A long time. We're almost done with our missions, aren't we?" Almandson smoothed his hair.

"He's t . . . t . . . trunky," Elder Perry answered, laughing. Jennalee knew the term used to refer to missionaries who were more than ready to go home, packing and repacking their trunks.

"I am not!" Elder Almandson said. "But it's true I don't like this place, and I'm getting married when I get home to Sandy."

The waiter arrived with menus and a corked bottle of wine with four glasses. The young people shook their heads vigorously. "No *vino?*" he asked.

"Oh no," Elder Almandson said. "We're Mormons, we don't drink alcohol."

The waiter clearly didn't understand. "*Signore*, this is the best of the red house wine, and is recommended with most of our entrees. Perhaps you would prefer white?" He spoke this in Italian.

"No, you don't understand. We don't drink wine. Water, please." Elder Almandson's face turned red.

The waiter shrugged one shoulder. "Bubbles or no bubbles?" This was in English.

"Once again, we're Americans, we don't like bubbly water."

Jennalee had been drinking fizzy San Pellegrino ever since she got off the plane, but didn't dare say anything. Terrilyn changed the subject as the waiter left shaking his head. "Why is Rome called the Eternal City anyway?"

Shy Elder Perry answered. "We . . . we found out it . . . was always . . . called that."

Elder Almandson butted in on his companion with a hint of scorn. "Ancient Romans thought no matter how many empires rose and fell, theirs would go on forever."

Remembering the history in her Blue Guide to Rome, Jennalee said, "And we all know what happened to the great Roman Empire."

Terrilyn smacked her gum one last time and put it neatly on her bread plate for later. "So what happened? I mean Rome's still here, isn't it?"

Trying not to gawk at the gray glob on the plate, Jennalee explained. "They fell, that's what. In the fifth century Rome was sacked by northern barbarians who threw statues of their gods in the Tiber River."

Elder Almandson smiled with confidence. "I know, but the barbarians kept Rome as a religious center, Sister, so it remains the Eternal City in a different sense."

"Okay, that's true," she conceded. "So here we are in one of the world's great religious centers and my question is: how hard is it to do the work of the Lord here?"

Elder Perry fidgeted with his fork. "You said it, h . . . hard."

"Not so fast. Sisters, have you seen our numbers?" Elder Almandson regarded them with his chin held high.

His cold managerial tone annoyed Jennalee. Not a word about the beauty of Rome, or its life-loving people. He covered his aversion with snide jokes. But she should be merciful, she thought, he'd probably been mocked and rejected many times here. Who knows how she'd fare as a missionary, half-hearted as she was? Would she sound like him in a few months?

"We'll see those numbers at the meeting in a couple days," said Terrilyn, her face shrinking behind the mound of spaghetti set before her.

"Sisters, it's under your watch that the new temple in Rome opens so your numbers should be phenomenal. All of central and southern Europe will use the new temple."

"Have you seen it yet?" Jennalee bit a breadstick. She knew a temple in Rome had been planned for decades but was shut out by Italian authorities. To plant a temple here was a major feat for the LDS Church.

"Yes, it's amazing, at least on the outside. It's to your advantage since people have such interest in temples here."

"We know all about it," said Terrilyn, "but thanks for the info." She wound long noodles around her fork.

The men tucked into their pasta, and it was a while before anyone spoke. Finally, Elder Almandson put his glass of water down. "And now let's talk about those female referrals. That's the real reason we're meeting." Jennalee didn't like the way he said 'female' but she knew better than to say anything to a priesthood holder. Missionary men were forbidden to talk to single women investigating the LDS faith, so it was up to the Sisters.

He handed a paper to Terrilyn. "Here's the address for a widow and her daughter living in the Trastavere section of Rome. These women will start your own numbers going, because you'll have a lot to do to keep up with us."

His bragging got old, she thought, knowing numbers could be fixed to look good. With this guy, pride trumped real concern for people. If they worked for the Spirit like they said at the MTC, it shouldn't be this way. Every tract, every Book of Mormon, every person talked to, and of course, every baptism had to be carefully spread-sheeted. It was an exact science, getting people to believe the LDS faith.

It was unreal how she was here to sway people, to gain converts from a populace that would overwhelmingly reject an American Church's gospel, not out of malice, but because their lives and faith fulfilled them. Latin culture outranked the Mormon way of life by thousands of years, so convincing descendants of people who traveled the same roads where Peter and Paul walked was a daunting task.

She wished she was free to experience Italy in its rich traditions with Alex, whose mother was from this country. He was somewhere nearby, in the vast Eternal City, and the thought consumed her. He'd left Utah so fast; maybe he was happier in Italy.

"We'll figure out how to get to Trastavere," said Terrilyn, "but can you tell us which buses go to Sister Agosta's place?"

Elder Perry wrote something down and handed the paper to her. "Fol . . . follow these directions to the Appian Way. You have to ww . . . walk a long ways."

"I think I know the bus numbers. So is the Appian Way near anything interesting to see?" asked Jennalee, hoping to see something interesting while on the visit to Sister Agosta's.

"The ancient Appian Way is near Ca. . . Catacombs," said Elder Perry, with a hint of a kind smile for her.

"They're not much to see, though." Elder Almandson sounded gruff. "Churches are built over the original sites with statues and paintings all over. But I suppose they are close to Sister Agosta's apartment so you might be interested."

"I th . . . think they're worth seeing," said Elder Perry in a low voice. "These Early-day saints were killed before the Great Apostasy, and we Mormons know what it's like to be p . . . persecuted."

Since she was a little girl, the very word 'persecution' brought up the deepest part of what it meant to be LDS. She'd been taught a terrible history of maltreatment and injustice no matter where Mormons wandered, like the Jews. Brigham Young led them to Deseret after Joseph Smith and his brother Hyrum were martyred, shot while in a jail cell.

"Those catacombs aren't anything compared to Carthage Jail," said Elder Almandson in a boastful way. "I've been to there a few times, and the tour is fantastic, but it's a sad sight to see the very room where our Prophet Joseph Smith was killed." Another pause and he bowed his head in reverence.

"You've been there?" Terrilyn sounded impressed. "I don't know if I could stand seeing it." Her voice choked.

Jennalee hesitated to tell them what she'd discovered but blurted it out anyway. "My dad's copy of Church History says there was a gun inside the room where Joseph and Hyrum Smith were killed. Did the tour guide say anything about it?" She knew she sounded contrary, but it seemed logical that if there was a gun, technically Joseph Smith couldn't be a martyr. Not if he shot back in self-defense.

"The guide never mentioned it. You saw that in the Church History book?" Elder Almandson folded his arms over his chest while the other young man gazed at the floor.

Terrilyn's cheeks reddened. "Sister, you do know the hymn, 'Praise to the Man' where we sing, 'he died as a martyr, honored and blest be his ever great name!' Don't you?" She sung the lines.

"In the second stanza," said the ginger-haired elder, "it says his blood was shed by assassins. There's no room for doubt. Brother Joseph was an innocent martyr. I think you misunderstood what you read."

Surrounded by hardliners, Jennalee knew questioning the story of the death of Joseph Smith marked her as a troublemaker but she couldn't help it.

"Of course I know the hymn. We sang it every Sunday during the bicentennial of Brother Joseph's birth. There was even a nativity scene set up at BYU Administration. Not for Jesus, but for the Prophet's birthday."

Terrilyn's eyes flashed. "Oh my heck, what are you talking about?"

"My mom and I went to see it while Christmas shopping. They had a scene with a little cradle from 1805 with baby Joseph in it and a fireplace, and a Christmas tree."

"It's true," said Elder Almandson, "because he was born two days before Jesus Christ, so it's reasonable to celebrate the Prophet's birth at the same time in the same way. And it was his bicentennial."

"Well, never mind. Just a few things to think about." Jennalee forced herself not to say another word.

Elder Perry, quiet until now, wanted more discussion. "You know, I heard the same thing, that Brother Joseph shot back and two men were killed. There were witnesses."

He'd lost his stutter with his random but bold statement. Unfortunately, his missionary companion crushed him with such a hostile stare, he was quiet for the rest of the evening.

They parted late, and outside the restaurant, they all shook hands. Jennalee caught the same stern glare from Elder Almandson that used to scare her whenever she saw the portrait hanging in her living room of her great grandfather Brigham Young, his flinty eyes looking into hers.

9

PUSHED TO THE LIMIT

Springing to his side in black dress and apron, Nonna handed Alex a fresh cup of coffee as he set to work in his uncle's home office. The rain outside contributed to his low mood, and he had to push himself to work on his contracts, since he'd lost the big one. Without a cell phone, he had to use the business line in the office.

Nonna put her hands on her hips, forcing his full attention. She spoke precise words with her southern accent. "Alessandro, I know you will not rest until you find the woman you lost. If you love her, you should marry her."

"I would like to, Nonna, if I can find her." His grandmother was different today, pensive and sad.

"When you find her, give her this." Nonna handed him an open velvet box. In it was a white gold ring with a large diamond surrounded with rubies. The stones winked at him even in the dreary light from the window.

"No, Nonna, this is yours. I saw it on your finger . . . when Papa was alive."

"You are the oldest of our grandchildren; I give this ring to you and the woman you choose for long life together like me and Papa."

"*Grazie*," he said, hugging her, "you give me hope but I don't think it's going to happen."

"This should give you hope, too." Reaching into her apron pocket, she took out a beat-up envelope and pressed it into his hand; a letter posted in Provo, Utah. The postmark was over two months old and his Kaysville address had been crossed out and replaced with their address in Italy.

On her way back to the kitchen, Nonna added, "If she won't have you, my Firenza will."

He gave his thin little grandmother a hug and she kissed him back before she left him to read it privately.

His smart girl had thought to mail a letter to his house. She *had* tried to contact him. He shook his head at the slowness of the postal system. Then, taking a deep breath along with a sip of strong coffee, he tore open the envelope.

> *Dear Alex,*
> *I hope you get this letter because I haven't been able to call or email. I don't know how everything got so messed up. After my parents grounded me, they changed my phone and cut off my Facebook. I tried to reach you secretly online, but you never answered.*

He'd lost his laptop, finally sent a message and then *she* never answered!

> *I had to take a mission in the Church to get away from Bridger. Brent knew the kind of pressure I was under and thought it was the best way to get away, but now I won't be free for more than a year. I'm in the Missionary Training Center and can't see anyone.*

Yeah, he'd found that out. His truck ate a whole tank of gas on the way to Provo.

> *My new address is below. I can only answer once a week. I wonder what happened to all our mail. Lost in cyberspace, I guess.*

Read by an old guy dating his mother.

> *In War and Peace, I read how Natasha broke it off with Prince Andre for the awful Kuragin. I'm not like Natasha, please don't think I am. They're sending me to Spain, so if you're still in Italy, you can come to Madrid and see me at the LDS Mission Center after the beginning of September. I'm in love with you, Alex. I won't ever forget you, even if you've forgotten me. Always yours, Jennalee*
>
> *P.S. I have no cell phone until I'm assigned. Then I share one with my missionary companion.*

She was the same wonderful girl. He was still in love with her, too. Jennalee wasn't guilty of not trying to reach him, only of being trapped by circumstances. The email snafu caused by Carl was a rotten shame, but there were people against them on both sides. Maybe she'd done the best she could under the circumstances.

Hearing her desperation, Alex typed an immediate response on his uncle's home computer, one full of love. With his girlfriend back in his life, his fears melted away. Nothing was impossible now that he knew Jennalee still loved him.

He determined to go to Spain ASAP. They'd have a little time together to decide the future. Alex took the ring out of the velvet box; it would fit her, he knew it would.

The business phone rang and Alex grabbed it, not noticing the Caller ID. "Enoteca Giovanini, *pronto*," he said.

"Alessandro, it is you?" purred a woman's voice, "I speak from your own phone, the one you forgot when you leave in such a hurry."

He put the ring back inside the box and felt his chest tighten, taking away his breath. His voice strained, he answered, "*Signora* Putifaro, mail my phone to me, if you would, please."

"We are much too busy with harvest to mail it. My husband gives you another chance. He signed your contract so you must come to our Abruzzo house to get it. I will give you your phone also. Exactly one week from today at four o'clock here . . . in Abruzzo. You have our vineyard's address."

Without a goodbye, Caprice cut him off and Alex was left talking to no one, saying, "I can't make it, I have to go to Madrid . . ."

He put the landline back in its receiver. Maybe it was a good thing she hadn't heard his last comment. He'd been given another chance with Largo; maybe things weren't so bad after all. The contract was signed and waiting. Driving to Abruzzo on a fall day to pick it up would be the highlight of his career.

His uncle, huffing, hurried into the room. "My briefcase, have you seen it?"

"Right there, Uncle Lucio, on the file cabinet."

"I'm so forgetful with this new business. I depend on you, Alessandro, you have a sharp young mind."

"*Grazie*, but hey, I'm not so sharp, Zio, cause I lost my phone. No worries, though, it's been found and I'm going to get it in a week. I'll have to check this office phone for my messages."

"No problem, as you say," said Lucio. "How is the Putifaro contract going?"

"*Signore* Putifaro signed it and I'm set to pick it up next week in Abruzzo."

"*Bravissimo*, Alessandro. Be cautious going to Abruzzo, won't you? It's a winding road through mountains. I've got to go now but I take you to lunch tomorrow to celebrate, yes?" His uncle left the room and Alex heard the Maserati start up and leave.

He tried to concentrate on his work, but he heard Caprice's husky voice in his mind. Could the messy incident with her have been totally forgotten by Largo? He still felt ashamed but tried to dismiss the bad memory, wanting only to think about Jennalee.

Alex glanced outside and saw the rain had ended. Putting the ring box in his pocket, he went outside and ambled up the road to clear his head. Harvest proved to be the busiest time in this business, and his uncle depended on him. How could he ever tell him about the strange episode at the Putifaro's house? Or even about going to Madrid?

Peeved by Caprice, he had to admit that being an adult in Italy was different than vacations here with his mom and Gabe. Carefree summers were a distant memory. He was now a player in international business. The fresh air somehow made him miss his dog, his friends, and even his old truck back in Utah. He kicked a dirt clod, knowing he'd have to put off going to Spain to see Jennalee.

Back at the villa, he slipped off his muddy shoes and went back into the office without motivation. He hadn't cracked open his Bible for weeks, but it used to help direct him. Leafing through the apps on his iPad, he found Olive Tree.

He opened to First Timothy Chapter 6, a passage that cut through him like the two-edged sword it was.

> "... People who want to get rich fall into temptation and a trap. . .
> For the love of money is a root of all kinds of evil. Some people, eager for
> money, have wandered from the faith . . . causing griefs. But you, man of
> God, flee from all this. . ."

He'd wanted comfort, some encouragement from God and this verse felt hard and cold. Wait a minute, he thought, his ears hot. Lack of money *caused* his grief! The crush of medical bills from his dad's cancer treatments *caused* his family to be poor. His mom wouldn't accept much help from her brothers.

Now that he had money, it felt good. With this high-class job, he was handed a chance to make some real cash. Why not strive for a high position in the export business, buy a great car, and skip college for a while? He closed the iPad with a frown.

The phone rang again. This time he checked the number. Unknown. "*Pronto, sono* Alessandro," he answered.

"*Buongiorno,* Alessandro," said Firenza, "won't you meet me for lunch this week?"

10

NO COMPROMISE

Silent days ensued at the Young home after Brent's announcement of unbelief. The younger boys hid out in the family room watching TV while their mother cried as she made dinner. Not one for harsh words, his dad hid his anger. Dad spoke often on his private line, the one in his study reserved for Stake President Business. They all waited for LDS authorities to make a decision about what to do with Brent.

A tattered Bible sat open on his desk upstairs. It had belonged to Rachel. The day she left Argentina to go home to Oregon, she said, "You need a readable, modern version of the Old and New Testaments, so I'm giving you mine. No worries, I have another one at home. Sorry it's marked up." She handed him a beat-up copy of the New International Version.

Obstinate, he still tried his line, "See, Miss Christenson, it's like I told you before: so many versions and translators corrupted the original."

Her voice quiet, she said, "God wouldn't let that happen, Elder. It might happen to any other book, but not his Word. I challenge you to read it. If you have questions, shoot me a text. I'll be ready." Her eyes twinkled.

When he'd opened Rachel's Bible at the tiny hovel of an apartment he shared with Ammon, the highlighted passages took on new meaning. He saw into a tender woman's soul by reading her own intimate communion with God, and amazement took the place of scorn. Here was a girl who highlighted Psalm 126: 5: *'Those who sow with tears will reap with songs of joy.'* The page held a watery wrinkle.

Rachel put exclamation marks at every point of Ephesians 6:10-18, a warlike passage for a petite woman like her, he thought. Her deepest thoughts were penned on nearly every page of the New Testament.

He resolved to read the New Testament straight through like she'd said, not just picking out the passages LDS used. As he did, it sounded so unlike any of the books of LDS scripture, he began to desire more of it. Reading it changed him, resulting in his present dilemma, with a 50/50 chance of being discharged with honor or dishonor, depending on the judgment of the bishop and others in the priesthood.

Rachel texted him and he opened her old Bible at her urging, to Matthew 10:17. With every religious table in his house flipped upside down, Jesus' warning blew him away in its precision.

> *". . . On my account you will be brought before governors and kings as witnesses to them . . . but when they arrest you, do not worry about what to say or how to say it. At that time you will be given what to say, for it will not be you speaking, but the Spirit of your Father speaking through you. . ."*

Would the Spirit help him? Brent felt guilty about humiliating his parents. Awash in uncertainty, he skipped a few pages and read Matthew 23:4. Jesus was describing the religiosity of the Pharisees. *"They tie up heavy loads and put them on other people's shoulders, but they themselves are not willing to lift a finger to move them."*

That Scripture, too, was spot on. Constant pressure of getting baptisms and converts crushed him in Argentina. At heated meetings, Brent would stare at his Mission President's polished cordovan leather tasseled shoes until they were blazed in his mind. His own shoes, and Ammon's, had slogged through the rain and mud of Buenos Aires and were far from shiny.

The President's official letter said he'd served honorably, but today could still go badly. Hiding his beliefs now would make him a hypocrite, and since he'd already felt like one during his mission, honesty and integrity had to be first. Sick stomach or not, he had to tell his bishop the truth.

His phone buzzed as he got into the car with his parents; he saw a text from Rachel. *I'm praying for you. You are not alone. Jesus is the only One you need.*

Could a born-again Christian like Rachel honestly have any idea what he was up against? She'd never had to be a temple-worthy priesthood holder keeping high and holy rules. Even if she didn't understand it all, her text gave him courage. He texted back.

No turning back, no compromise. Thanks for prayer. I can feel it.

"Quiet your phone," his father demanded, "don't your friends know what you're doing today?"

This friend knows, he wanted to answer, but he silenced the phone. A terrible thought assailed him: he had split up his forever LDS family. Only when all members stayed within Joseph Smith's teachings could they be together forever, and he'd spoiled it. But he'd never wanted to hurt his family, or even the Church. Then a counter thought came to him. Wasn't his religion and maybe all of them . . . weren't they specifically designed to keep their people inside?

They got out of the car and Brent offered a shaking hand to his bishop. His tie choked him. The bishop escorted him into his office and shut the door.

"You have no idea how many phone calls I've had with your father." Bishop Crosby, about his father's age, had an imposing presence. He indicated a chair for Brent, while he sat behind his ornate cherry wood desk. "First, let me ask you what you learned on your mission."

"Well, sir, I learned to understand scriptures in a new way."

"Go on."

"I learned how to serve the poor. But I also learned the rich think they don't need God. I learned that people don't want religion, they want relationship with an all-powerful God."

The reddened fury on the bishop's face spoke for him. "Excuse me, Elder Young, that's not what I meant."

"You asked me what I learned, sir, and I haven't yet told you the greatest thing I learned."

"The greatest thing?" The bishop kneaded his hands, his elbows on the desk.

"Yes, sir. I learned how much God loves me and I'm saved by the one and only Jesus Christ and His Cross."

Shock on the bishop's face turned to stone in the next second. "Your father warned me about this." He clasped his hands together and stood up. Brent tried to stand too. "Remain in your chair," he said, pointing a finger at him.

Bishop Crosby paced the room and preached at him. "What about your belief in the only true restored gospel, the one you were on a mission to share? Ours is the only Church on earth that pleases God, the only one!" The poor man got red-faced and took his jacket off in spite of the air-conditioning. If he has a heart attack, Brent thought, I won't know what to do; he wished Eagle Scout Ammon was here.

"You haven't yet spoken about Joseph Smith, who as a boy of fourteen saw the Father and the Son in the sacred grove. What about the Book of Mormon, the most correct book on the face of the earth, brought to us by the power of God and his Prophet? Speak to me of it and your belief in God's Living Prophet, who is the only one on this earth authorized to speak for God. How dare you not believe, Elder Young?"

The same words he'd heard over and over again throughout his life made him realize how dead they were. He desired a Living Word, sourced in a loving God. In the background, the drone of the bishop's words became fuzzy, but clear as a bell, a still small voice in Brent's head told him to stand firm.

So he stood up and standing strong, he said, "You say I don't believe in these things. You're right, I don't."

The man's chin jutted out as he got next to Brent's face and grabbing his lapels, pushed him back into his chair. The bishop towered over him, glaring down in a position of power. "Did you tell your father all of this?"

Brent said nothing.

"Elder Young, what you are saying borders on apostasy and you know what that means. I've done it before, I can do it again."

Brent knew the word well. *Excommunication.* "I'm aware of this, sir, but I'm still not ashamed of my testimony of Jesus."

His bullying stance disintegrated and the bishop sat down at his desk. He put his head in his hands. "Where did you go astray, Elder? Your mission President tells me you led an praiseworthy life in Argentina, and never got out of line. He gave you an honorable discharge."

Brent kept silent.

"So, for your father's sake . . . and against my better judgement, I will discharge you. Elder Brent Nephi Young, you are released from your full-time mission." He slammed his hands on the desk.

"Honorable or dishonorable, sir?"

"That remains to be seen. Elder Young, you . . . are . . . the firstborn of five brothers, one already thirteen and in the Aaronic priesthood. You are their example."

"Yes, sir."

Again, he pointed a stubby finger at Brent. "Your next step will be Sunday when you report to your ward. If you don't perform to my expectations, I can and will refuse you an honorable discharge."

Outside, after lots of hand-shaking, he and his parents got into the car and went home. "So it will all be decided Sunday?" whispered his mother once they got home. He nodded. His father, on the phone again, didn't say a word to him.

Brent went back up to his room to wait for Sunday sacrament meeting at the ward chapel when his phone rang.

"Hi, Brent," said Rachel, "how'd it go? Are you in a lot of trouble?"

11

FRIENDS IN HIGH PLACES

Jennalee opened her email in the internet café near the oblong Piazza Navona in the center of Rome. After waiting for months for a word from Alex, a message appeared, just like he'd never lost her. Her heart skipped a beat as she opened it.

> *My Jennalee,*
> *Got your letter! It's from way back in July. I can't believe we lost so much time. Long story, but Nicole told me you were on a mission when I tried to find you at BYU a couple weeks ago. I'm still working in Rome. One-year pact or not, I have to see you, so I'm coming to Spain ASAP. Email me as soon as you get this. I love you, too. Don't ever think otherwise. Alex*

Spain? Jennalee sat dumbfounded, trying to remember her letter's contents, written before her assignment changed. Heat spots broke out on her neck when she thought of Alex going to Madrid. She typed an answer furiously. Only twenty minutes remained in her allotted time to answer the rest of her mail from supervisors, friends, Brent and her parents.

■ ■ ■

At the same moment, only two streets from where Jennalee typed her answer, Alex stretched his six foot frame at a covered outdoor table at the Ristorante Tre Scalini in the Piazza Navona. Summer tourists had gone home and the Piazza was less crowded as he reviewed his iPad. Dressed in a European fitted navy suit and open collared rose-colored shirt, he fit in with business people on their lunch breaks milling around the cobble-stoned square. He'd even slicked back his unruly curls with Italian pomade which he thought made him look older.

He read another word of encouragement from his pastor in Utah. His inbox showed another email as he closed out Pastor Ron's without answering it. JYoung? Could it be? He'd given up and now here was something from Jennalee, sent mere minutes ago.

> *Alex, don't go to Madrid! They changed my assignment to Rome! Can you meet me at the Piazza del Popolo fountain at noon tomorrow? I'm with a companion 24/7, so you have to pretend you don't know me. I just want to see you. We're staying in a room on Via Margutta. If you're not there tomorrow, I'll wait until next week. I'm always yours, Jennalee*

She was *here*. Jennalee had entered his life again, center stage, and God had to have orchestrated it. He stared at the message, hardly able to breathe with the rush of emotions from months of no communication. She still had to be online, so he started to type a few words to her.

Just then a scent of expensive perfume made him look up, right into the languid eyes of the statuesque Firenza Tarentino, early for their lunch date. Of all the times to show up early, he thought, swallowing complicated feelings of guilt, but he stood up and held out a chair for her.

"*Buongiorno,*" she said, sliding into it with grace. "I hope I am not disturbing you?"

"*'Giorno,* Firenza, *momento,* I'll finish this up." He glanced at his few words, wishing for time to send more but knowing he had to cut it short.

I will be there. C U noon tomorrow. Love, Alex

He slipped the iPad into his briefcase with reluctance, knowing Jennalee was still online. But when he saw how pretty Firenza appeared in her pink linen dress and matching shoes, his good manners kicked in.

"Tre Scalini is a fine restaurant, do you come here often?" A little small talk; maybe it would cover his excitement about Jennalee in Rome.

"I come far too often, it's a bit boring," she said, with a half-smile, "but I thought since you had never been here, you might like it very much. The food is superb."

With her rippled blonde hair unleashed, Firenza resembled the Renaissance woman Botticelli painted, but today, he only had eyes to see his Utah girl's straight blonde hair and sky blue eyes. His hope to see her nagged at him to get through this lunch. He saw a blonde walk by, and thought she was Jennalee, and when she wasn't, he had to cover his disappointment.

"You seem distracted," said Firenza with her strange smile.

"I'm sorry," he said. "What wine do you recommend?"

"You will see."

A waiter came and gave them menus. "*Grazie*," Firenza told him, nodding at Alex. "We'd like the usual wine, *per favore*." The waiter had it in hand and poured the red wine for them before returning for their order.

Lifting her glass, Firenza spoke in a low voice. "To your health and that of your grandmother."

Alex lifted his glass. "And to you and your family," he said, sipping the wine. "It's the best, Firenza," he told her, surprised at the complexity of the elite Amarone della Valpolicella from Veneto. He'd never had it before. If this was her house wine, she had awesome taste.

"Alessandro, your grandmother's fine meal in the villa's garden was something special. Not many people have such a wonderful family," Firenza said, "nor one so large."

"*Si, grazie*, I'm grateful to have them, especially Nonna." He sat taller, knowing she respected the distinction of his family's three-hundred year-old house outside Rome. His thoughts of Jennalee would have to wait. He couldn't find an excuse to leave, anyway.

He ordered the Roman specialty, *spaghetti alla carbonara* as did Firenza. Their talk was of light subjects: weather, vineyards, and family.

"I've been here almost every summer since I was born," said Alex. "How did I miss meeting you?"

"I went to a Swiss school, remember? Even summers, I stayed there."

"It must've been hard for you, away from home. Were you unhappy there?"

She took a little breath. "Unhappy? It was normal for me and I had many friends. Here I have only my brother and father and they are busy with the family winery. Always so busy."

Firenza's lovely hair caught a breeze. She wasn't the ice queen his cousins implied, not if she appreciated his noisy family. They ate the pasta dish in Italian time, and the hour passed with Firenza warming up with talk of the wine business. She knew far more than he'd guessed about the world. Jennalee moved from center stage in his thoughts . . . at least for now.

Lunch ended and Firenza flagged down the waiter for the check.

"I'll get it," protested Alex, feeling strange about her paying for him.

"I will let you take me to another restaurant another time," she said, "I invited you, remember?"

Feeling the wine, he appreciated generosity. "Firenza, thank you for a delicious *pranzo*. The *carbonara* was the best I've had, and the wine you chose, excellent." It'd been some of the most expensive wine in the vault. He'd have to remember it when he took her out next time.

"*Prego*," she said, "I wanted to see you again and you were so good to come, Alessandro. Our next time together will be your choice."

The song '*Volare*' played from the café's hidden speakers as they left their outside table and strode toward Bernini's statues in the piazza's central fountain. *Volare* meant to fly; how he wished he could. The strong wine made him feel a little dreamy.

"Our flat is off the side street over there," said Firenza. "But you can see our building best from the other side of the piazza."

High-end residences like these were out of his price range. Alex saw her with new appreciation. Her lifestyle didn't skimp on the extras. "How do you like living in the center of Rome? It'd be great to live next to my favorite piazza."

"Which is?"

"This one, Piazza Navona."

She nodded. "I like it, too. Alessandro, you are . . ." She stopped. "Ah, here's Salvatore to take me home." Her voice faded as she watched her dark-haired brother striding towards them from the direction of their flat.

"Firenza, I get a feeling your brother disapproves of me."

"Not at all. Salvatore is just . . ."

"Be honest with me. Does he dislike many of your friends or just Americans?"

She shrugged. "He is protective, but be assured, Alessandro, he likes most everyone after he gets to know them. You are my friend, so he will like you, too."

"Yes, I am . . . your friend. I actually heard from my. . ."

He couldn't believe he was about to tell her about Jennalee. Maybe he shouldn't. Firenza would never have the occasion to meet her anyway. Salvatore's shadow crossed his face where he and Firenza stood by the fountain. From his little side smile, he could tell her brother relished interrupting their conversation.

"*Buongiorno*," he said in a loud voice to Alex, shaking his hand with a strong grip. "You enjoyed the famous Tre Scalini?"

"*Molto bene*. Very much."

"Your family's party was so fine, my sister keeps talking about it." Firenza's face reverted back to a cool countenance. What was it about those two? She was a classic beauty people stared at, but right then, she didn't shine. Her brother, though handsome, had dark brooding eye brows like storm crows across a gray sky.

"Are you ready to go, Firenza? We must take father back to Veneto this evening. He doesn't rest well in the city." Salvatore's bass voice resonated in spite of the noise from the fountain.

"I hope your father feels better at your country villa," Alex said, taking a deep breath to fight sleepiness after the pasta and wine. "I must go, I have a business appointment at the UniCredit bank." He tried to impress

Salvatore by mentioning the large European bank; he knew he was striking a pose, but couldn't help it.

Salvatore looked past him directly at Firenza. "We bank there also. Perhaps we will see you as we settle some financial matters before we leave the city." The men shook hands but Firenza said *ciao* with a soft kiss on his cheek.

Alex watched them hurry away as he put on his sunglasses. He swiped an escaped curl back into place and headed for his favorite building in Rome, the Pantheon, before his bank appointment. How confusing it all was. He hoped the peaceful atmosphere under the ancient Roman dome would help him think.

12

A FUNNY THING HAPPENS ON THE WAY TO THE BANK

Lunch with Firenza proved more fun than he'd anticipated and she'd become a friend, well sort-of. She needed someone like him to talk to while escaping her domineering brother. And Nonna knew more than she was telling; he'd make her spill more of Firenza's story as soon as he got back to the villa.

Whenever he was in Rome, Alex loved the adrenaline rush of breaking out of a narrow side street suddenly landing in front of a major monument. Today the Pantheon filled his view, the two thousand year-old domed masterpiece of architecture. Even with its pocked exterior, it took his breath away every time he saw it. Once a temple dedicated to all the gods, it had been converted into a Christian church in recent times.

So Jesus had won out, he thought, against Rome's multiple gods. Reverence replaced restlessness as he entered through the giant pillars and stepped onto the colored marble floor, buffed smooth. Voices echoed in muted velvet tones and sunbeams wafted down from the skylight, raining peace in a church with no dark corners.

His job wasn't as fun as he thought it would be, except for the Maserati. Uncle Lucio trusted him to handle all the pressure but Alex wondered how he could live up to that expectation. He began to think life was simpler as a Starbucks barista driving an old truck around Utah with his girlfriend.

Last night he studied a few Scriptures like his mom suggested, and concluded wine wasn't forbidden in the Bible, but getting drunk was. Wine was a daily cultural experience in Italy; it was a non-issue. He concluded it was okay to continue being a sommelier. But did he actually like this life?

Alex groaned inside. It stressed him out to think his uncle wanted him to sign for a loan, opening himself up to the possibility of having to repay a large debt. No problem, Uncle Lucio told him, the bank only needed another signature and the loan would be repaid long before he'd have to chip in. In the few remaining minutes he had, he walked outside to stand in the coolness of the Pantheon's ancient portico with its granite columns to reflect on it all. He reached into a pocket for his phone, forgetting. Waiting to meet Jennalee was sure to be an agonizing twenty-four hours, and when they did meet, he'd have to pretend he didn't know her.

His eyes were still adjusting to the deep shade when he saw a pair of young women standing near the center obelisk dressed in knee-length skirts. Americans for sure, he thought, with those practical shoes instead of the high heels Italian women favored. He squinted.

The way the blonde one stood was utterly familiar, but her hair was shorter than Jenn's. Warmth rushed to his head as he moved toward them to see more clearly. He reached the blonde girl whose back was to him, when she made a sudden step backwards. Alex bumped her arm and a book flew from her hands.

"*Scusi*," she mumbled, bending to pick it up. He saw her perfect ear, with the pearl earrings she always wore. She turned, shaking her hair, framing the unforgettable face.

A stab of joy pulsed through him. "*Signorina* Young, the fault is all mine, I should've picked it up for you like I did last time."

"Alex?" she whispered, glancing around for the other missionary. "I can't believe it."

"Me neither. Your hair's short and I didn't recognize you . . ."

"You're different, too. A business guy, very cool."

"Warmer now that I see you." He noticed the other LDS girl taking a group photo of some students. "Is she your companion?"

Jennalee nodded, not smiling.

"I . . . I missed you." Knowing he was stealing time, he took her in his arms and kissed her. After all, he thought, this was Italy, where they were like any other couple in a romantic rendezvous. Well, it would be normal except for the official LDS nametag with *Sister Young* on it.

When they parted, Alex saw those lively eyes dance on the innocent face of the girl he'd left in Utah months ago. A little breathless, she said, "Alex, be careful."

He laughed. "Don't worry, I will. How is it we meet here accidentally, right outside the Pantheon? What are the chances?"

"Alex, she'll see us, so don't do that again, or we'll be caught."

"You loved it, Jenn, but you're right; I understand your position," he said in a hurry, "my plan to play the investigator goes into effect . . . as of now."

Glancing at her still-occupied companion, she forced him to stand at arm's length where they pretended to peruse the volume she'd dropped, a blue Book of Mormon.

Alex inched closer. "How long have you been here?"

"Barely a week, I have a lot to tell you, Alex, but here she comes."

Pretending to be a stranger demanded endurance after the long lapse in their relationship. He wanted to embrace her again, talk for hours, and hear the entire story of the last few months. Instead, he had to pretend to be a possible convert to Mormonism. He really had been an investigator once, so he knew how to play the part. Heck, last year at school they'd discussed their separate faiths many times; this was nothing new.

"Have you ever read the Book of Mormon?" she asked as her companion approached.

"*Sorella* Young," he whispered, his eye on the other girl. "Tell me about it." He warmed to this role as an accomplice to her subterfuge, forgetting all about his bank appointment.

The missionary companion moved to their side the next instant, speaking rapid Italian. "*Buongiorno*, I'm Sister McKay. Sorry I was busy helping those students from Korea, and you are. . ." Her Italian was perfect, maybe even better than his; the MTC had done its job.

Alex held out his hand. "Alessandro Giovanini, *piacere*. I speak English." Using his mother's maiden name in case she'd heard his real one, he shook her hand with fervor.

Jennalee's neck, splotched with tell-tale red marks, gave away her nervousness, so he covered for her by stating, "Your sister tells me great things about your Church of Saints."

"You speak English so well, *Signore* Giovanini. An American accent?" Sister McKay was a plainer girl than Jennalee, but cute in a pinched sort of way, with brown hair and a narrow face.

"I like to practice my English with Americans." Alex tried to appear innocent, but put on dark sunglasses so she wouldn't see him relishing the image of Jennalee beside him. It was important to pull off this game without getting caught.

"We can make an appointment to talk more with you about our faith. Do you have a family?"

"My uncle is here in the city; we own a wine shop. Yes, please, an appointment to meet again," said Alex, "but today, I know a *gelateria* near here. I will . . . how you Americans say . . . treat you?"

Sister McKay, a smidgeon pudgy around the middle, glanced at Jennalee, who nodded. "Okay," she agreed.

"Best *gelato* in this part of Rome," Alex said, thinking he would burst with this small talk when all he wanted was to be alone with his girl and clear up the months-long lapse in communication. They walked across the piazza where a long line of people waited at the popular corner *gelateria*.

Minutes later, when they were third in line, Sister McKay excused herself to go to the restroom. "You stay here, Sister Young, since you can see the door and *Signore* Giovanini will need help with the *gelato*. Get me cantaloupe flavor."

"*Si, Signorina*, I will get it," Alex said. "Can't . . . elope?"

He saw Jennalee couldn't suppress a smile. "*Melone, cantalupo*," she translated for him in front of Sister McKay.

"Ah, *molto bene*, I like it, too." Alex grinned.

"I'll be right back." Sister McKay walked across the scrubbed tile floor to the back of the *gelateria*.

As soon as she left, Alex bent down close to Jennalee's face, and moved her hair back with his hand. Tears built high in her blue eyes, about to tumble. "Are you okay?" he asked. "Jenn, you were supposed to meet me in a year but now you're on a mission?"

"For eighteen more months," she said. "You have to believe me, Alex, I'm not in this because I want to be. And God helped me find you today. That was . . . what I prayed for so it's not all a loss."

Tears or not, Alex wanted her to own up to what she'd done. "It's frustrating, Jenn. You're stuck like glue to this other girl for the next year and a half. How can we even talk? How can this work?"

"We'll see what happens. God can do anything, Alex."

Her face softened with no sign of the frustration he felt. "So you got my letter at last. What happened to our emails?"

"A tangled web," he explained, "with a meddler thrown in."

"A meddler?"

He told her as fast as he could about Carl. "He tried to fix my mom's worries, I guess. You should've heard my mom break up with him over it; she's gutsy."

"I guess my parents aren't the only ones who don't want to see us together. So how does your mom feel about me now?" Her softness held an edge.

"Mom feels mega bad about the whole thing and she's on our side. She even prayed for me to find you. Listen, we've got to meet tonight, Jenn."

"It would mean sneaking out after Sister McKay's asleep. Totally against the rules." A sharp edge overtook her voice. No matter, he loved hearing it again.

"Wow, you're here. In Italy." Alex relaxed. "There's so much I want to show you."

"I always wanted to go to Italy with you, remember? Not quite what we had in mind though."

"I'll take it," Alex answered, "we'll figure something out."

"When I heard you were on the BYU campus, and I was stuck in the MTC, you don't know how sorry I was that I missed you."

"So your mission is because of your parents?"

"Partly. They thought I was straying away from the faith and pressured me to get married."

Alex's voice rose in spite of trying to keep calm. "I heard. To Bridger? Your parents sure don't like me."

"Wouldn't your Mom have done the same? I mean, if she saw you straying away from *your* faith? Besides, with Carl messing up our email, it's about even, don't you think?"

"You're right. Mom would do anything to keep me on the straight and narrow, only she did say I was free to make my own decisions with her guidance, of course. She's not keen on me driving all over Italy in my uncle's fast car either."

"Do you?"

"Do I what?"

"Drive a fast car?"

"Jenn, it's a Maserati. I sure wish I could give you a ride . . ."

They stepped to the head of the line and the clerk stared them down to hurry the order.

"*Un cantalupo, un riso, ed un cioccolato.*"

While Jennalee kept an eye on the bathroom door, Alex set the ice cream cups on a table. No Sister McKay emerged yet and they sat down next to each other at a table for four.

"Have I changed much?" she asked.

Enjoying their closeness, he locked eyes with her. "Not on the outside. Short hair or not, you'll always be gorgeous. But your nametag with the *Sister Young* . . . what a shock. . ."

She blushed. "That's on the outside. I haven't changed inside. Not that I didn't struggle with you being gone, but I take it as a miracle we met in the middle of Rome."

"When I met you in Utah, I took it as a sign, too, but Jenn, you and I have serious problems, this being one of them." He touched her nametag like it would bite him.

"Didn't you always say 'God will make a way where there seems to be no way'?"

Alex swallowed. "You're quoting my mom."

"Well, God did put us together in a way we never could have seen."

"Except a choice needs to be made, Jenn."

"I know," she said, shaking her hair.

"Hey . . . Sister's headed this way." Alex moved his chair a few inches. "Jenn, you've got to meet me at the Giovanini wine shop. It's on the Via della Croce, close to where you live on Via Margutta." He slipped his business card into her hand. It also had his cell phone number, the one held by Caprice Putifaro. "Um . . . don't call my cell though . . . it's lost." He wasn't about to go into *that* story.

"Alex. . ."

"Midnight at the shop."

She nodded just as Sister McKay arrived at the table, glaring at Jennalee. With an ingratiating smile, Alex handed her the cup of cantaloupe *gelato*.

"*Sapore di cantalupo, Signorina.* My pleasure."

"*Grazie,*" said the dour young woman, sitting across from Jennalee.

"So crowded," smiled Alex, "only this one place to sit."

"I see that," said Sister McKay, "it was crowded in the bathroom, too. But, *Signore*, we have strict rules about being alone with men, and she's breaking them." She gave Jennalee a nasty look.

"Alone with me? In this crowd?" Alex gestured with his hands. "You Americans are . . . what is the word? Puritans?"

She made a face at him. "Thank you for understanding our rules; I can see you are a gentleman."

"*Sì, Signorina.*" Alex changed the subject. "Sister, I hear your religion builds a new temple." He needed to divert her.

She perked up. "How did you know? It's open soon for public viewing, and when we get the announcement, Sister Young and I will guide visitors inside."

"I see it in *Il Messaggero*, the paper; new buildings interest me, I'm Roman."

Sister McKay blushed. "We could accompany you if you'd like a tour . . ."

Jennalee found her voice. "You understand, *Signore* Giovanini, after the dedication it's closed to non-members, so you have to see it before that date." Her companion frowned at Jennalee for a second, then in the next instant, faked a smile.

Alex thought he'd tease Sister Sweet and Sour. "So outsiders cannot go inside because of secret animal sacrifices?"

She reddened. "You have it wrong, *Signore*. It has nothing to do with animal sacrifice. Temples are sacred, not secret. We make covenants with God there, and if we keep them, we are blessed."

"What covenants?" Alex had limited knowledge of Mormon temples, so his question was for real.

"One covenant is marriage, when we're sealed to our spouses . . . for time and eternity." Jennalee spoke, holding his gaze.

"I hear of marriage made in heaven, not of marriage *in* heaven." He almost lost his Italian accent on that one.

"We believe the way to Celestial Heaven is a marriage sealed in the temple."

Alex tried to keep a casual tone, ignoring Jennalee's intensity. "You say marriage is the *way* to heaven?"

Sister McKay took a turn. "The highest heaven, the Celestial, is the reward for all those who seal their marriages in the temple."

Alex wanted to be adverse. "Millions of people all over the world marry without this sealing."

Sister McKay snorted. "Maybe, but a temple wedding is reserved for the best. Who wouldn't want a forever family?"

Annoyed, Alex blurted his real thoughts. "But, Sisters, in the *Vangeli di Matteo, Marco, and Luca*, Jesus says there is no marriage in the afterlife." He felt Jennalee's pale eyes steady on him.

Sister McKay was oblivious. "*Vangeli?* We have the restored gospel, so what it says in those gospels doesn't matter, our scriptures say different and they are correct."

It doesn't matter what Jesus said? Alex had to get up and throw away his gelato cup, he was so angry. Sister McKay followed him, saying, "It's not hard to join us. Once you're baptized you can enter the temple."

This bossy little woman wanted him baptized. He pictured her dunking him underwater a bit too long to punish him for his disbelief. No matter what, she was bound to ruin his reunion with Jennalee. There would be no way they'd be able to play this game much longer with the dogged persistence of the missionary with all the answers.

His stomach did flip-flops by the overtones of the conversation. Did Latter-Day Saints really believe being married in their temple got you into the best heaven? So marrying outside the temple meant . . . what? Did Jennalee believe this? If she did, why would she ever marry him?

The three walked out of the ice cream shop with Alex in the lead. He took off his suit coat, carrying it over his shoulder, his briefcase in the other hand. "You see before you the Pantheon, temple of all gods. In Rome, we have hundreds of temples and your church builds one more. Why do we need another temple? Do we need a Christian temple instead of a church?"

Sister McKay answered. "You don't understand. We are Christian but not Catholic or Protestant. We are the actual restoration of the true Church of Jesus Christ. And we need a temple for our sacred ordinances. I told you before."

In this circular argument, Alex almost lost his cool, and closed the discussion. "Then you are in the right city, *Signorini.*" He made a wide gesture with his arms. "This is the Eternal City where the cross of Jesus made a holy church from a pagan temple. As you see, the Pantheon is now a church."

Sister McKay had nothing to say for the first time that day.

He glanced at his Dunhill watch. "I must go. Won't you walk with me to my bank?" Alex had long since missed his appointment, but he would try to sign the loan papers anyway.

As they walked, Sister McKay was distracted by a large bus stop area. "This is where we catch our bus, Sister Young. I know it is."

Alex pointed across the street. "It would be there, next to the sunken ruins. I am sorry for knocking the book out of your hands, Sister Young, and I am glad to meet you both." He scooped up their hands and kissed them, turning on the Italian charm.

Jennalee spoke up. "We'd like to give you this Book of Mormon, and perhaps we will see you tomorrow at noon? At the Piazza del Popolo?"

"*Sì*, if I can, I will be there."

"We can teach you more about the importance of the temple and answer any questions," said Sister McKay.

"I have a question, Sisters. Are you nuns or do you both have the same first name?"

Jennalee clucked her tongue with a disapproving tsk, tsk. "*Signore* Giovanini, we'll have to watch out for you."

Alex didn't want to let her go. He mouthed, "Meet me" but only got a slight nod from her. With one backward glance, he waved and headed to the bank, hoping he'd get there before it closed but wondering if he should.

■ ■ ■

"*Signore* Giovanini is strange, but handsome as all get out." Sister McKay chattered on as they waited for their bus. "I'm not sure we'll be able to move him through the steps to baptism very fast. He likes to argue."

Jennalee sighed. It was excruciating to leave Alex and follow her companion. After accidentally meeting him, some of her worries melted away only to be replaced with a new crop. Alex was upset about her mission, but she knew God had a plan.

"*Ciao*," he'd said, waving and smiling in that crooked way of his. From across the street, she watched as Alex leaped the steps to the bank entrance, his suit coat slung across his shoulder. He was different than he'd been in Utah, confident and sophisticated, but he'd always be her Alex, wouldn't he?

Out of nowhere, a woman in high heels hurried to where Alex was on the stairs and converged on him. From way across the street, Jennalee saw her standing tall in a pink dress, her long blonde hair rippling in the breeze. She must have been nervous or excited, since she twirled her sunglasses in her hands.

As Jennalee watched, they talked a minute and then the woman had the audacity to kiss Alex on both cheeks. The fashionable woman walked back to the curb where a taxi waited for her and Alex disappeared inside the dark doors of the bank. Tonight she would have to talk to him about this . . . woman. She felt hurt and angry all at once.

"Stop staring into space, Sister, our bus is here," snapped Terrilyn, "and tie your shoe!"

13

BRENT'S PRICE

The neighborhood ward expected Brent to give a full testimony for his homecoming at their local chapel. He resolved to tell them only what Jesus led him to say, knowing that a few true saints, in their mercy and kindness, would always regard him with honor, no matter what.

His poor mother tried to appear normal, hiding in public what had to be major pain. He'd inflicted torment on his parents, not realizing the full cost of his decision. There was no intent to dishonor the church or his family, but he would never be sorry for choosing Jesus. Waves of overwhelming love for his parents poured over him; love he knew came from God.

The bishop and his father conferred in a side room before sacrament meeting. When Brent was still strong in the LDS faith, he'd heard these two men boast of their perfect lives. To them, perfection was keeping a temple recommend, fulfilling a calling, doing a mission, and following every duty outlined by the Prophet to achieve the highest place in the afterlife, Celestial Heaven.

But he'd never felt worthy. In Argentina, acute feelings he was a failure before an angry LDS God assailed him every night. The enormous eye that seemed to follow him from the spires of the temple held him under its scrutiny. Still, he hadn't lived life without his Church and he didn't know how to.

The gymnasium in the center of the chapel that also served as the Sacrament room filled up with families. Almost time. Chairs scraped on the floor as people chose seats. Mothers in dresses held babies while herding toddlers. Proud fathers hushed their broods of children.

He straightened his tie and tried to ignore his nervous stomach. Brent knew each family. They and this place were a part of him, his life, and he would miss them. The bishop had strategically sandwiched his speech between several other speakers since it was 'Fast and Testimony Sunday'. As he sat through the others, he was so distracted, he didn't hear them.

"Elder Brent Young." Calm, he walked up to the microphone. He cleared his throat, hoping to speak clearly.

"As you know, I've returned from my mission in Argentina. In First John 5:11, John says, '*And this is the testimony: God has given us eternal life, this life is in his Son. He who has the Son has life.*' This is my testimony, too. I testify Jesus is my Savior, he lives in me and he alone makes me perfect. Thank you for being involved in my life while I was growing up and for your kindness to me here and on the mission field. I will never forget it. I love you all and will continue to obey God in all I do."

His words pierced through the room. He bowed and waded through the quiet to sit in his chair, flushed and hot. Had they noticed how much of the testimony he'd left out? Then his brother Boston applauded, then his mother, and all his brothers. Soon, everyone clapped for him, smiling. It was over, and come what may, the bishop had to realize everyone in the ward seemed to approve. Now his fate was in God's hands, no matter what the bishop decided.

■ ■ ■

"Ammon, I got an honorable discharge. I don't know how, since my bishop thinks I'm apostate. You won't have to worry about it, you're not like me." The almost-brothers were on the road from the airport to Price, Ammon's home town.

His two-year companion listened with a serious face and Brent could tell he didn't understand taking such a bold step, risking his temple recommend and his standing in the Church. "How are your parents taking all this?" Ammon asked, "I mean, it has to be a shock to them."

"They're upset, but I think they'll get used to my new life eventually."

"I hope so. Brent, I don't know what you went through in your mind in Argentina, but it concerns me now." Even though his friend stood strong as a Latter-day Saint, he was no rat and had never reported Brent's deepest voiced doubts.

"Thanks for sticking by me, through all my mental craziness. Don't worry, I'm okay with God and I can't explain it, but I am closer to Jesus than I've ever been before."

Ammon closed his eyes in the passenger seat. Brent knew he couldn't deal with this conversation and changed the subject. "Enough about me, tell me how your dad is doing."

"All I know is . . . he's in a coma in the hospital. The accident happened at the coal mine he's worked at for twenty-five years."

"I remember you got the news that he hit his head?"

"Head trauma, by falling in front of a moving coal car. It's bad though, because my mom lost her job last year and my three sisters are still in school."

"So you aren't going back to BYU?"

Ammon shook his head. "Not yet. Sorry, we did have plans to room together." Disappointment in his voice stung Brent.

"No worries. I'm not going back either, not to BYU anyway."

"Brent, you have college all paid for; you've got to finish your degree. Weren't you trying for law school?"

"It's all up in the air now. I didn't even talk to my father about it. First step for me is to take you home and then I'll see what's next."

Ammon was silent, then said, "You didn't tell me you had a BMW."

"A graduation gift from my parents. German engineering is top of the line." He felt spoiled, knowing that Ammon's family would never be able to buy such a car for him.

"I'd be taking the bus if you hadn't picked me up at the airport, now I'm riding home in style. Thanks, Brent."

"I couldn't let you go home on a bus; we rode enough buses in Argentina after our bikes were stolen, remember?"

Ammon smiled. "When the plane landed, I felt like kissing the ground. But I'm coming home to . . . so many problems."

Brent's mood saddened; his own charmed life had always been financially secure. Besides the college fund, Grandpa Young had left him a sizable amount to go on a mission, and there was plenty left until he decided what to do. He resolved to help his loyal friend.

"So are you quitting the Church, Brent?" The question reverberated in the car.

"I don't know. I just want to see what it feels like not to go to Church for a while, to just read and pray, and go where God leads. I want to learn more about the Bible so who knows? I may take some classes."

He could tell Ammon felt uncomfortable and didn't know what to say. A wall formed between them. Brent adjusted his Sirius radio to a station he'd been listening to all week. "Good to hear American music, isn't it?"

A sign indicated the ramp to Spanish Fork which headed east to Price. "Have you heard this station before?" They listened to the words.

"It's about Jesus," Ammon said, "reminds me of Alison and Rachel's music, remember?"

"I remember." The music had a major part in helping to open his spiritual eyes.

"The best time on the mission was working in the orphanage with those Christian girls. They had something . . ."

"Hey, I'm still in touch with Rachel, she's going on another short mission. She calls it Why-Wham or something."

"Ask her to tell Alison 'hi' for me." Poor Ammon, so shy with girls.

"I could get her number for you."

He shook his head. "I'm too busy. I didn't get as close to her as you did to Rachel, you know."

"Didn't think you noticed."

"C'mon, after being with you for two years? I picked up those love vibes." He laughed. "I hope . . . I hope it works out, Brent, but I seriously don't know."

Brent ignored his remark. "So maybe I'll go to Portland to catch up with Rachel at some point."

"That's where Alison is, too, right?"

"Yeah." A silence broke their camaraderie.

Ammon spoke quietly. "I have good memories of them, but they're way different than us."

"You didn't say much during those conversations."

"I got confused, Brent. I needed to study the Scriptures more."

"What are you talking about? You studied more than I did."

Ammon said, "Everything but the Bible. It unsettles me. I have a feeling it has deeper things in it I know nothing about."

"Me, too. And I didn't know anything about the Bible until I talked to Rachel. I told you what she said helped get me out of my depression."

"Yeah, but I don't know, I have to concentrate on helping my mom and sisters. I have to stick with the Church, Brent. It's all I have."

"I know."

"Don't get me wrong. Our experiences made me wary of some things the Church teaches, but for now, I have to put all doubts on a back burner, and just believe."

"It's okay, Ammon." Brent drove further in silence, then asked, "So how many wards are there in Price?"

"The whole of Carbon County has about fourteen."

"Wow, that's a lot of Mormons."

"Would you believe we have a Greek Orthodox Church, too?"

"More than we have in Kaysville. So do you know any Greeks?"

"'I went to school with a few. One of the girls lives down the block from us; they kind of keep to themselves, though." Ammon looked thoughtful. "But I know why. Greeks are a minority here like we were in Argentina."

"Yeah, Argentina changed *my* whole perspective."

"Me, too. I mean . . . I saw it before, but I didn't *feel* it."

"Did you ever think the 'norm' in Utah isn't normal to other people? Like, the rest of the world drinks coffee. And wine and beer. They don't have to wear long underwear all the time."

Ammon cracked a grin and shook his head and they listened to the radio as the road climbed through the red-willowed canyon. Reaching Soldier Summit, a windswept flat plain, they got out at a tiny store and gas station.

"Need to stretch our legs," said Brent, putting on his jacket. A red-tailed hawk cried overhead, balancing tipsy wings on the unsteady wind.

Ammon surveyed the bird's silhouette above them. "You're as free as the hawk up there, Brent, but I won't ever be like I was in Argentina."

"Hey, you're off your mission, Ammon. Who could be freer than that?"

Ammon shook his head, then studied the convenience store's window. "Hey, you think they have some *Dulce de Leche* ice cream like in Argentina?"

They tried to find it but had to settle for freezer burned ice cream sandwiches. Ammon swallowed his in a few bites on their way back to the car and threw the paper into the wind. "See, Brent, I honestly don't want to go home. Does that sound terrible? I don't want to see how bad things are."

Brent wanted to cheer him. "It can't be that bad once we get there, Ammon. I'll be there with you. After you take care of things, we could take a little vacation. Go to Portland or something."

"No, Brent, it's way worse than you think. My mother told me my dad gambled and got worse after I left. Sometimes he drove to Vegas and would be gone for a whole week. He thought he drank in secret, but we always knew because most of his paycheck was used for alcohol. This has been going on all my life. Now he owes a lot of people a lot of money."

"In two years, you never told me."

"And as if that weren't enough, he's in this coma. If he dies, he'll leave us with all his debt. If he lives, we still have it." Anger was a new side of Ammon he'd not seen.

Brent didn't know what to say. "People wake up from comas."

"You didn't live with my dad. I hate to say this, but maybe it's . . . better this way."

To break the mood, Brent set Sirius radio to the country western music he knew Ammon liked. He commented on the scenery as they came down from the summit. This part of Utah was new to him. When they passed a coal mine and he noticed seams of black coal in the hills next to the road, he tried to ask Ammon about it, but his friend was still in no mood to talk.

They pushed on and entered the small town of Price on the western slope of the Rockies, with green hay fields in the midst of a desert. Here, Otto Carr lay comatose in the hospital and was unaware of his son's return from a mission.

Sundown shot orange light over the Carr family's house and driveway as they parked. Only later did Brent see how driving to Price propelled him toward God's purpose for his life.

14

SLOW AS A SNAIL

Sneaking out that night would be tricky, but Jennalee needed to find out who Alex's 'other woman' was, the one who kissed him in front of the bank. Jealousy didn't feel right and she hoped her suspicions were baseless, but Alex looked so troubled. Something was wrong. Even with all their talk about God putting them together again, they were further apart than ever.

Back at the room on Via Margutta, she slipped into bed fully dressed under her robe while her roommate read from the Book of Mormon. Under the covers, she studied Rome's labyrinth of streets in her Blue Guide to find the exact location of the Enoteca Giovanini.

How ironic that the shop was on Via della Croce, the 'Way of the Cross'. Her mood softened when she remembered the silver cross pendant Alex had given her as a Christmas gift last year. She pulled it out from where she hid it beneath the undergarment she'd worn since the endowment ceremony at the Temple.

The whole episode about the cross was a major misunderstanding of their two cultures. Alex had been hurt when she reacted with shock at his gift. He didn't understand that LDS rarely wear crosses and that she couldn't wear it, at least not in public. She held it, her fingers wrapping around its cold silver, thinking of Alex with anxiety. In

Utah he'd been sincere and gentle; in Italy, he was pressured and edgy. She sniffed, and tucked it back under the sweetheart neckline of her garment.

"Sounds like you're getting a cold. Lights out," said Terrilyn at exactly ten-thirty.

"I'm okay."

"I feel like *I'm* getting one." Terrilyn blew her nose into a tissue.

"Hope not," Jennalee said sincerely, wondering how much whining her companion might do if she were sick.

Lying stiff and afraid for a long time on the twin bed, Jennalee finally heard Terrilyn breathing in a pattern. After arranging pillows to resemble someone sleeping, she crept down the hall to the bathroom where she hung her robe and put on her shoes. The family that owned the building didn't hear anything from the back rooms as she opened the front door.

On the street, groups of strolling young people laughed and talked. Via Margutta was busy with people after sundown. Most were headed for the nightlife in the piazzas, but Jennalee focused on reaching the Via della Croce, where the Giovanini Enoteca's light illuminated the door.

Alex opened the door to her knock, wearing casual jeans and a T-shirt, his hair once again wild and wavy. He looked like the Utah Alex again and she found it hard to be angry.

"*Benvenuta!*" he said, his arms open wide.

"What a welcome," she said, slipping into his arms. They kissed for a time and his smell, his warmth, felt like home again.

When they parted, Alex opened a cold bottle of San Pellegrino bubbly water and poured it into wine glasses. They sat at stools behind the glass and wooden counter of the shop. He pulled a paper out of his pocket.

"While I was reading the Book of Mormon you gave me, I found this. Your phone number, addresses, the works. Thanks."

"I wanted us to be able to contact each other for once."

"Yeah, right? I'll keep it till everything changes."

She wasn't sure what he meant. Then the ugly nagging thought of the other woman rose up in her.

"Is everything going to change? I lost you once, when I was back in Utah and you were here," she said. "Then I come all the way to Italy and I've lost you again."

"What do you mean? We just found each other."

"You found someone else." She felt her voice quiver.

"Jennalee, I don't have anyone else." He frowned, his face serious.

"What about the tall blonde woman outside the bank? The one who kissed you?"

He hesitated. She'd definitely surprised him. "You must mean Firenza. It's not what you think. She's a long-time family friend. She came to Nonna's birthday party at the villa and asked me to lunch today."

"Must've been some lunch."

"Those are the only times I've seen her. Oh yeah, and the third time in front of the bank."

"An accidental meeting, I imagine. She certainly likes you, Alex."

"There's nothing between me and Firenza, Jenn. You know Italians kiss each other goodbye."

"Usually it's more of an air kiss." She took a deep breath and resolved not to accuse him further. Only could she trust him? "I believe you, but you're different, Alex."

"And what about you, Jenn? Taking on a mission? You've changed your tune." She remembered his quick temper. He still lost it once in a while.

"I admit my parents control me, but I can't let them down."

Alex calmed a bit and told her about seeing her brothers. "Your brothers were so cautious with me; I caught the drift they don't like me. They told me I interfered in your family. Guess so, huh?"

"For my part, it was good interference, Alex."

His lopsided smile reappeared. "An interesting development I found out while at BYU is that Nicole and Bridger are together . . . well, sort of. I think it's more on her part."

Jennalee whistled. "Nicole can have him. Marrying him would've sealed my fate."

"Hey, this gentile gets it . . . sealed in the temple to him . . . for eternity. Wow."

She shuddered. "You don't know how hard I tried to get away from people setting me up. Bridger's father wants a trophy wife for his son because he's running for State Senate. I'm a Young so I guess that matters to him. It doesn't to me."

"Well, in Utah you do have a pedigree. Got to marry high there."

"Alex, I don't care about that life any more. I just want you."

He looked away. "I'm nobody in Utah, Jenn. I lived in a rented house and worked at a coffee bar. But here . . . my family owns a three hundred year-old villa with a producing vineyard that gives me great paychecks." His voice took on a hard tone. "Our house is older than the United States."

She swallowed. "I'd love to see it, Alex, but I never cared that you didn't have much money."

"Back there, I never felt good enough. It's different here. So yeah, maybe I have changed."

She'd never seen Alex this insecure or concerned about money and didn't know what to say.

He stood and paced the tile floor, putting the counter between them. "I went all the way back to BYU trying to find you, worried you were with that . . . *idiota* and find out you're on a mission. No matter what I do, you are unreachable."

"Hey, you don't need to call him an idiot. Why don't you believe I can't stand him? I did all this to stay with you."

"I don't get it. What are we going to do with you on a mission?"

"I'm aware of the problem, Alex, but you're the one who went off to Italy the day after graduation for this job."

"You were supposed to meet me in May, Jenn, and I missed you so bad, I was going to break the pact when I went back to find you and. . ."

"It's a mess, isn't it? And because I'm stuck here, I can't see my brother Brent who went home the same day I came here."

Alex grunted. "Wow, how cruel. I don't get all these missionary rules. I'm not a member but I'm already tired of them."

"Can't you see I've never lived a life without rules? Obedience is everything to us, and I'm not disobedient."

"Until now."

"Right." She reached over the counter and smacked his arm. "It's all because of your interference, you fake Italian, Alessandro Giovanini. It's your mother's maiden name, isn't it?"

He lightened up and smiled. "Yes, I thought she might have heard my real name. So how *is* your brother?"

"I'm worried. Brent doesn't act like he did before his mission. He met a girl in Argentina, and I think he got serious. Things aren't so great at home. He wouldn't stray from Mormonism though. "

"Maybe that *is* what's going on at home; his girlfriend isn't a Mormon, like me, the interferer."

"You could be right."

"And he might be questioning some things."

Maybe Brent *had* gone through some of the same doubts she had. "If I'd known going on a mission would hurt our chances this much, I would've just run away, Alex."

He softened and put a finger to his lips. "If you mean that, come with me to a place where we can forget all this."

She followed him to the back door which opened to a courtyard shining with moonlit white jasmine. Fingers of violet bougainvillea dripped from the ancient stone walls and fragrance filled the night air, as the blossoms sent out sweet signals before the coming of cooler weather. A slow running fountain sparkled with pearly water.

"I'll be right back," Alex said, disappearing into the darkness before she could say a word. Jennalee felt apprehensive, like he'd gone to a place she couldn't follow. What was he up to anyway?

She sat on an iron bench and saw a land snail climb up a pot of geraniums, its shell on its back. It would travel so much faster without a wobbly shell, she thought. But how could it give up its comfy home with all the neat compartments?

Alex came back with cushions to throw on the iron loveseat. Then, striking a long match, he followed brick paths to light candles, some in glass jars on the ground, and some in iron stands. When she saw the effect, even Temple Square could not compare to this secret twinkling garden under the moon in Rome.

"Alex, it's so . . . exotic." In the flickering light, they snuggled together on the softer loveseat.

"Let's sit here and just be together." He put his warm arm around her, but she shivered.

"Wait," he said, getting up. When he came back, he brought a red pashmina shawl. "A customer left it in the shop today," he explained.

Jennalee wrapped it around herself and leaned against him, watching the fountain's glittering water pour from an ever-filling urn. She hoped nothing else would ever come between them.

"Alex, I'm afraid of all this change. It's hard to accept things not staying the same."

"Yeah, our lives sure changed after graduation. More than I thought."

"I wish I could get over this feeling that I have to be so perfect. With my father as Stake President, I live in fear of doing something wrong."

"They need to allow you to live your own life, Jenn."

"Easy for you to say. You're a guy. Daughters are different, and I came to a place where I was either going to oppose everything my parents stood for or do a mission."

Alex kissed the top of her head. "Sorry. I'm trying to understand."

"So now, I'm going through the motions, except I'm not really living. You know what I mean?"

"I do know," he said. "It's hard not to try to please the people you love. I do it, too; I'm doing it now with my uncle."

"Just when I have a vague feeling I'm on the right path, someone raises the hurdle just as I run up to it." Jennalee squeezed his hand.

"I hope you're not talking about me."

She laughed. "Not you so much as the Church. As for you, God's going to have to knock me on the head before I figure out what I'm supposed to do."

"Not too hard, I hope." When he said it, she could tell he was smiling.

The candles flickered around the fountain as a soft breeze rose and she tightened the shawl around her. "I want to stay here forever with you. It's like heaven tonight."

"Unfortunately we both have responsibilities. What about your mission?"

"Oh, that. Do you think you can wait for me seventeen and a half months?"

He halfway groaned. "Don't know, I was kind of crazy when we couldn't communicate, and that was only for three and a half months."

"Me, too."

"Hate to ask, but when do you have to be back?"

"Terrilyn sleeps like a log and I know she didn't see me sneak out."

He laughed. "So that's her name? I call her Sister Sweet and Sour."

"How mean, Alex." But she wanted to laugh, too.

"Haven't you noticed how her face goes from sweet to sour in less than a second?"

"Mm, true. Hey, my watch says twelve thirty; I can stay another hour."

"So we have plenty of time."

"What do you intend to do with all this time?"

"Oh, by all means I intend to 'choose the right'. I totally respect you, Jenn, but get me alone with you in a garden in Rome and who knows? It's hard to stay away from you."

"On that note, we'd better walk around," she said, standing up.

He still sat, gazing up at her, still holding her hand. "Mostly, Jenn, I can't believe you're here. What we have . . . a lot of people search for all their lives and never have. And yeah, we're young, but if you can't be in love when you're young, you might miss it altogether, you know?"

She knelt and took both his hands as he sat on the bench. "We still have it, don't we? We're still impossibly in love."

"Impossible is the action word." Candlelight reflected in his eyes.

She shook her head. "Hey, I won't accept that word even though I've used it myself. Being in Italy, and knowing you grew up here in the summers makes me feel so much closer to you, Alex. There's wisdom in the way they live here. It's what I dreamed of, an ancient place with deep roots. Older-than-America roots."

He stood up and hugged her. "It honestly is the sweet life, most of the time." In the moonlight and among flickering candles, he kissed her until she could hardly breathe.

"Whoa," she said, moving back.

"Sorry." He took a step away. "You don't know how I felt when I recognized you in the piazza today."

"Right after going out to lunch with Firenza in her high heels?"

"Who's jealous?"

"I guess I showed up in the nick of time, before she took my place."

"Hey, yeah, how *did* you swing coming to Italy for your mission? Don't *they* tell you where you're going?" He took one of her hands and they walked a stone path together.

Speaking of miracles. . ." She told him how sudden the reassignment came.

"Jennalee, don't you see? This is God telling us we're meant to be together. If this is His signal, you need to quit your mission."

She sighed. "Easy for you to say. I don't go back on my promises, even if my heart isn't in it. Or even if I was getting away from Bridger and my parents."

The moonlit garden fell silent. She knew he was unhappy with her.

Alex spoke first. "In my eyes, you exchanged a promise to me for your obligation to the Church."

"Well, to me, it puts us off a few months, that's all, Alex. You know I'm bound by duty."

"You're letting it come between us."

"We can still see each other."

"You're unavailable, and I'm too busy to play an Italian investigator. It's like you're in jail and I'm visiting."

She didn't know what to say, not wanting their time together to end in a fight. "Do you work at this shop every day?"

"Twice a week; the rest of the time I drive the Maserati to wineries. I'm making a ton of money in the export business."

His voice was faint when he answered, so she asked, "But do you like your job, Alex?"

He let out his breath. "To tell the truth, I'm in pretty deep and there's a lot I don't like about this business, but my uncle depends on me. I guess I'm bound by duty, too."

"So we're both stuck and the pressure's on."

Alex tightened his mouth. "Not only that, I made an enemy. Long story, but a contract's riding on it. I can't tell my uncle until I fix it in a couple days. Sometimes I wish I'd gone straight to college with you. Not BYU, of course."

Reaching under her sacred garment, she held out the silver cross for him to see.

"You kept it after all," he said. "You're even wearing it." Alex took her by the hands and kissed her hair.

"Of course I am, it was a precious gift from you. I'm sorry I didn't realize it at the time. I want to know Jesus like you do."

"I bet you're the only LDS Missionary who wears a cross," he said. "Better than your long underwear, don't you think?"

"Alex, don't mock us. But mine are kind of itchy. Too much polyester." She tucked the cross back under her collar.

"Why do Mormons have to wear them?"

"They remind us of covenants promised in the temple. Also, they're protection against temptation and evil."

"Oh, that's how you got away from me so fast."

She laughed. "They might come in handy for that situation but I have to wear them next to my skin until eternity."

"No, you don't."

"Well, that's what the Church says. That's what I vowed . . ." Bucking rules made her uncomfortable.

He reached for the chain around her neck and pulled the cross out. "You're wearing too many badges. You only need this cross and even if you lose it, it can be engraved in your soul for eternity, no temple ordinances necessary."

"But what if . . . my Church is partly right? I can't lose what's right in it."

"I don't know, Jenn. They do have some things right."

"You can't 'throw the baby out with the bath water' as they say."

"No, but as I see it, it's a close imitation of the truth. And truth mixed with untruths is confusing. I get that, but did you forget how much you wanted to be free of religious rules?"

"I'd die of guilt, Alex. I have to serve this out or completely humiliate my parents who love me. I promised, took solemn vows. You wouldn't believe what happens in the . . ."

Alex blew his long curls away from his eyes. "In the temple? I probably wouldn't believe it. I have a question for you, Jenn. Which Jesus got you here, the Mormon one up in heaven and way too busy for you, or the personal Jesus who loves with unconditional love?"

Two different ideas of Jesus; she could see that. The Savior she'd grown up with was 'an exalted man' in LDS doctrine. Could it be possible to know . . . to truly know the Jesus of the New Testament like Alex said? But what about sin?

"In the training center, I was made to feel miserable for every bad thing I ever did or thought. I heard Army boot camp is like that, tearing you down to make you into a worker to spread the Church's beliefs."

"I worried about you there; I thought you'd come out as a super Mormon. Do you think you can get past it to have a future with me, Jenn? I didn't tell you, but my uncle paid my ticket to Utah. He wanted me to find you and marry you and bring you back to our villa."

Jennalee's pulse raced. "What? So fast? I mean . . . *marry* me?"

Alex's calm face was sincere. "I would've done it, Jenn. But I'm not temple worthy so we'd have to elope or something. I mean, you'd miss getting married in the temple wouldn't you?"

She felt tears and sniffed. "Alex, let's not talk about it. I was raised to marry in the temple. That's the most important thing for an LDS woman. But I realize now it isn't all there is to life."

"So, maybe, we could . . . someday, I mean . . ."

"Maybe, nothing is impossible with God." They both paused until Jennalee said, "I want you to know I'm reading the whole New Testament, Alex, all four Gospels and the Epistles."

His Adam's apple went up and down as he swallowed. "Wow, Jenn. I've been so busy, I haven't read the Word for a while."

"Alex, you're the best thing that's ever happened to me, but I can't leave right now. I want to leave, I just can't."

He inspected the stars in the dark blue sky. "If you did, we'd be to-gether on my job because you'd help with the business. Nonna would teach you to cook Italian. You'd wake every morning in the countryside and take a walk on a lane lined with cypress trees and acres of grapevines. Most days we eat outside under a pergola."

Alex's pleas began to persuade her, but if she left, would she be a snail without a shell? Her default had always been her parents, her upbringing, her Church. How could she change that drastically?

"Give me time to think, Alex." And she would, constantly.

"The night is young. C'mon, let's hit the city." They went back through the shop and he locked the front door, pulling down the clattering green shutter at the entrance. Holding hands, they strode toward the Piazza di Spagna where music could be heard a block away.

"You Italians sure like to go out on the town late," she commented.

Alex led her to an ornate marbled building. A discreet sign revealed a McDonald's restaurant was inside.

Oh . . . the memories of the Golden Arches sign. "I miss having break-fast with you at McDonald's on Gentile Street," said Jennalee.

"Unlike that one, this one has marble floors and frescoes," said Alex. "They tried to make it extremely Italian."

"Want something?"

"We could go to a more refined restaurant if you're hungry."

"Let's just eat here for the memory. I miss the fries, don't you?" She found a place to sit as Alex went to order. She was happy for anything to remind her of home, but she knew she shouldn't be here; the clock showed one o'clock in the morning.

"McDonald's Italian-style," said Alex, setting down a tray of food.

He unwrapped a burger with pancetta on it. "I don't come here much; my clients like fancy places."

She didn't smile. "Not good enough for *Signorina* Firenza?"

Alex frowned and stole one of her fries. "Drop it, Jenn. How can we be together when we can't *really* be together?"

"Heavenly Father has a purpose for this, I know He does."

"How are you going to do the mission? I mean, do you still believe in it?"

"I don't say much, Terrilyn does most of the talking. In the MTC, I did have to put my mind on hold about what I discovered last year. I mean when I read the Book of John."

Alex looked tired. "I've put spiritual things on hold, too, for this job." He raised his voice under the fluorescent lights. "But what happens when we do that? We have one foot in, and one out." He took a small brown crispy fry and crunched down on it.

"I don't know, Alex." She was a little afraid of his mood.

"Listen, Jennalee, I'll speak for myself. I need to be all in for Jesus. It's weird otherwise, almost like . . ." There was a long silence and they looked away from each other.

"Like what, Alex?"

"Like he's not there," he said so low she could barely hear him.

She could see trouble on his face as he walked to the door, leaving most of the food on the table. Grabbing the fries, she stuffed them in her pocket and went outside with him.

"I'll walk you home. It's late and I have meetings tomorrow. Tell Sister Sweet and Sour I texted and can't make the noon meeting. I won't keep playing the fake Italian, Jenn."

"I know."

"Don't text or call my cell yet, okay? I have to pick it up day after to-morrow. Another of my many problems."

They walked off a side street leading to Via Margutta, and Jennalee held his arm tighter. "Alex, I'll sneak out again tomorrow night."

"Fine by me because if you're caught they'll kick you out."

"I won't get caught. But I do have to see you, Alex."

He spread out his arms. "Well, Toto, you're not in Utah anymore and Italy is waiting to be discovered. Only you've got a leash on you." He put his forefinger on her shoulder where her nametag had been.

"One more night, Alex, tomorrow we can decide what to do, how to continue. . ."

After the magical experience in the garden, his kiss was too quick in front of her door. "Meet at the wine shop tomorrow night, and I'll have a surprise for you. Good night, Jenn." She watched as he walked away under the lamp light. Their lives were so complicated and something was wrong, very wrong.

15

BLESSED ARE THE POOR IN SPIRIT

"Sister Young, I can get my backpack myself," said Terrilyn, at the entrance to the Vatican Museums the next day.

"I'll carry it upstairs for you," said Jennalee, shouldering the pack with her companion's water, food and LDS books. "I know you don't feel well, and the staircase is a long climb."

"How do you know?"

"It's in my Blue Guide to Rome. Bramante's staircase winds up and up like a spiral."

"You're right, thanks. I can barely breathe with this cold in my head."

Tired as she was, all Jennalee could think about was Alex. How long could they continue to discuss issues with no solution? She sensed a crisis; they had to resolve it tonight.

With permission from their mission President to tour Rome, Jennalee and her companion chose to visit the Vatican, the center of Western Christianity. The LDS Church wanted them to know the historical background of the country they were sent to convert. Holding museum passes, they headed up to view miles of Vatican treasures. As Jennalee climbed the stylized ramp with double backpacks, she couldn't help but think of the snail of the night before, climbing up to nowhere, heavy and slow.

Because the Vatican had a ruling against proselytizing, they were without their badges identifying them as Latter-day Saints. It was only fair, thought Jennalee, since it would be like Catholics trying to convert Mormons on the grounds of the Salt Lake temple.

"I can't believe all these riches," said Terrilyn, once they were inside. "See all the gold and silver candlesticks and stuff? Why don't they sell it and give it to the poor?"

Jennalee had an answer. "Wouldn't it be a great loss to the world if they did? This museum has centuries of human history." The Blue Guide had said as much.

"But don't you feel sorry for all those poor beggars out there?"

Jennalee had seen them alright, loitering near the Vatican Walls, beggars of a kind not seen in America. One man scooted around on a board with wheels because he had no legs. Others had skin sores. Jennalee wished Jesus was here to heal them.

"Such suffering people," Terrilyn said, "so I gave a tract to every one of them."

"They need hope and healing, not just religion or money."

"Well, I did my best." She was cranky.

At four foot eleven, Terrilyn was a stubborn dynamo of Mormon virtue. She'd worked in the temple from the age of twelve. In Italy, whenever a person yelled at them or called them names, her attitude grew even more superior and defensive. It fast became a chore to be with her, and now Jennalee was doomed to go through the Vatican with her on a day when she was in turmoil about Alex.

"Sister Young, what do you think about our new investigator, Alessandro?"

"What about him? I told you he said he couldn't meet us today, didn't I?"

"So defensive. He sure likes you. Too bad he's a wine merchant." Terrilyn had such a sly attitude sometimes.

"It's his job. Everyone has to make a living."

"A shameful one if you ask me. Are we going to tell him the Church forbids alcohol?"

"You go ahead, because I don't see how he or any Italian would change. They'd laugh in our faces. I don't know if you noticed but I haven't seen one person drunk here, and I've seen many in Utah. Just saying."

"Oh well, we have to turn him over to the Elders anyway. We're not supposed to be talking to a single male."

"He cancelled this meeting so apparently he's not interested anymore." This was getting surreal, all this talk about Alex's fake Italian persona. "Let's visit the Raphael Rooms. We can't be here and miss some of the best High Renaissance paintings."

After seeing the painter's enlightened artwork, she spotted signs pointing to the Sistine Chapel with its famed ceiling by Michelangelo, an even greater artist. Jennalee made a beeline towards it with Terrilyn tottering alongside.

"Is that the entrance?" she asked.

"Too small of doors." Terrilyn answered.

"Well, it used to be a private chapel, not meant for all these people."

They joined the line. People carrying binoculars talked too loud and she wanted to shush them. The crowd pushed through the tiny door into the high-ceilinged wonder of the world where a security guard told them to take no photos or video. No one listened or obeyed.

With Terrilyn feeling weak, Jennalee found a bench for her companion, who then waved her away. "Go ahead, I'll just sit here and watch our backpacks. I'm not interested in art, anyway."

So Jennalee wandered around and surveyed the ceiling until her neck ached. As one masterpiece after another illustrated the Bible, her comfort zone began to fall away. The painter had a passion for movement and rendered these paintings as though he believed everything in the Holy Book.

She glanced at Terrilyn, who seemed like she was asleep. Moving further into the chapel, she found herself saying '*Scusi*' often.

Alex had seen this place so she tried to look at it through his eyes. No wonder the LDS painting he saw in the local ward chapel surprised him. It was from the Book of Mormon and he'd never seen anything like it. She was starting to realize Mormonism was a small sect of Christianity, with a theology that was troubling.

She walked until she faced the altar wall with the blue sky of the restored Last Judgment painting. An English speaking tour gathered and she squeezed into the group led by a lanky young man dressed in black. He signaled with his hand for silence, pausing before he spoke.

"Welcome. From medieval times to the Renaissance, only the educated could read. The purpose of Christian art was to explain the Bible to the illiterate and to inspire holiness in those who could read." He coughed then continued.

"The Sistine's themes are about where we come from and where we are going. This work was painted twenty-five years after the ceiling. I think you can see right away why it's a groundbreaker. Almost everyone is naked. The artist removed clothing to disassociate each person from their social position, so they're on equal terms before Christ, rich or poor, saint or sinner."

For Jennalee, the painting was hard to look at. The ceiling was moving and lyrical, but this picture was harsh and in-your-face. The terrorized faces on ugly bodies was not a nice subject for church, she thought.

She remembered a soft and gentle picture of the same subject in her ward chapel with Jesus in his heavenly white robes welcoming people among white clouds. She couldn't help wondering why they were so different.

The art historian continued, "Here you see St. Bartholomew, one of the Twelve Apostles, holding his skin to show the manner of his martyrdom, but notice the face is not his but Michelangelo's. Was he showing his own repentance here?"

Jennalee lost focus, regaining it only when her ears tuned in again. "Here we see what the artist did to one of the critics of this work. He painted donkey ears on him and placed him in the lower corner of hell." Everyone laughed.

"The Apostle Paul writes that you came into this world with nothing, and you will leave it with nothing; including your clothes." More nervous laughing.

"So whether you're with the blessed rising up on Christ's right, or on his left, among the damned forced down to hell . . . all you have in the end, is your life in Jesus."

The young man paused. "Seeing this, we must reflect on Jesus's most important question: 'Who do *you* say that I am'?" He paused and closed the tour with a thanks for their kind attention. The young man dressed in black slipped away, leaving the crowd studying the lower depths of hell rather than at the blue heavens.

She was doing her mission for Jesus not only the Church, wasn't she? A kind of panic seized her as she wandered back to get her companion. If she did all the right things the Church said and lived a good life, it should be enough. The words of the art historian made her feel afraid. Did she have to be 'all in' for Jesus as Alex said?

"What's the matter? You look sicker than me," Terrilyn whispered, raring to go. "I'm outta here; I mean this is the place they choose the Pope."

Jennalee tossed her head. "The Pope? Don't we have a mouthpiece of God in Salt Lake City? We just call him a Prophet."

Terrilyn stopped in her tracks. "Sister Young, our religion is about as far away from this one as you can get, and for good reason. How can you even begin to compare our Prophets to *their* clergy?"

Jennalee shrugged. Pride emanated from her companion like the wrong kind of fire. On the way out, they passed the young guide on a chair in the hallway, taking a break before his next tour. Jennalee's discomfort returned. She wanted to ask him: *How exactly do you give your life to Jesus? What does it mean?*

Terrilyn nudged her. "He's a hunk, but unavailable."

"Hey, Catholics get married. Why do you say he's unavailable?"

"The black collar and clothes mean . . . he's a priest, isn't he? Maybe a beginner priest or a monk. What a waste, staying single your whole life. And totally against the restored true gospel as we know."

Jennalee tensed. From what she read in the New Testament Gospels, heaven wasn't about marrying, but it was useless to tell Terrilyn about it. "I just thought the black collar meant he was a worker or something," she muttered.

The intense young priest's face was seared in her memory along with his words about Jesus and the Last Judgment. Marriage wasn't the primary means of gaining heaven, was it? Because that guy knew about getting to heaven.

Exiting the museum, the girls blinked at the autumn light in St. Peter's Square. For lunch, they bought Panini at a kiosk and ate them under the huge columns, dodging pigeons who flew in to eat the crumbs. They walked around the Square and Basilica with its circular colonnades. It felt much like Temple Square, only gargantuan in size and hundreds of years older. The temple was a miniature in comparison. Jennalee felt she was on holy ground, though very unfamiliar holy ground. Nothing she'd seen that day matched her theology.

What if . . . Jesus wasn't a literal flesh and bone son of Heavenly Father and Mother in the pre-existence? What if he wasn't a spirit brother of Lucifer? It would change everything she'd ever learned about Jesus. But the Son of God she'd seen today pictured in the paintings were of a bigger, more powerful Jesus.

They passed the Swiss Guards and went inside St. Peter's Basilica. Birds flew around the lofty ceiling, so far upwards it made her squint to see them. Shafts of sunlight poured through the highest windows. The building was so large, it took them a few minutes of walking on the marble floors to reach the vast dome. There they lingered, listening to echoed sounds. The stillness added to the prayerfulness of the place.

"We're not even members but they allow us into the holiest place they have." Jennalee spoke in a hushed voice.

Terrilyn huffed. "We're not allowed up *there* by the altar, the holiest of holies."

"We can get closer to see it; there are no veils."

"I think it's spooky in here."

"Maybe it's because you're not basilica worthy."

"I am temple worthy though, and so are you, but you won't be if you keep talking so . . ."

"Shh, Sister. This place inspires us to be humble and holy. I mean don't you feel like an ant? The sheer size of it makes me feel small."

Terrilyn plopped herself down on a bench. "You can walk around here by yourself. You're the most uncooperative companion I could've been stuck with." *Ditto*, thought Jennalee, escaping to the front center of the basilica with its twisty wooden columns.

Above it was a golden circle window depicting the Holy Ghost as a dove. The stained glass bird was backlit with rays of sunlight that energized her soul. She knew she had to keep searching to find the truth. The challenging day ended with a sun-filled gentle Spirit smiling down on her.

Terrilyn appeared at her side. "I have to go to the bathroom, and you have to come with me."

16

STANDING AMONG RUINS

That night, after Terrilyn took her cold medicine and started to snore, Jennalee tiptoed out of the apartment for her second midnight date with Alex. It got easier, this slinking around the rules. She could hardly wait to tell him that after visiting the Vatican, she was closer to finding a life outside of Mormonism.

She ran to the wine shop on Via della Croce which she found shuttered, completely closed. More sad than angry, she looked down the street for him. Parked a few doors away was a guy in a leather jacket and helmet sitting on a Vespa scooter. Alex? He'd promised something special, she thought, just as he waved and held out a helmet to her.

"Hop on," he said, as she approached.

"So is this is my surprise?"

"One of them. Rome's amazing at night, you've got to see it."

Taking the helmet, she stuffed her hair into it and climbed on the back. "Okay. Isn't there an old saying 'When in Rome, do as the Romans do'?"

Alex accelerated, and they were off. Her arms automatically went around his waist, and it all felt so right. She was rewarded with the free feeling of flying on the back of his bike, clearing her confusion.

Alex drove to the ancient Forum, lit up in a glory of temples and columns, still standing after centuries. They circled the giant amphitheater, the Coliseum of Rome, the last place many martyrs saw before they died.

"How many people did it hold?" she yelled at Alex.

He glanced back. "Fifty thousand! All free of charge!"

They couldn't talk much; the noise of the bike shut out their voices. The eerie lights around the Coliseum beckoned like a wanton woman for entertainment in the form of bloody violence for all. She'd read how Roman politicians provided 'bread and circuses' to gain power over the population. She shuddered without being cold.

Stopping at the Piazza del Spagna, Alex led her to a cozy café with yellow light behind arched windows. The inside was candlelit with curved brick ovens lending aroma to the atmosphere of warmth and charm. She spoke in Italian. "Is this where you bring your Roman girlfriends?" She was only teasing, but he was in a serious mood.

"I'm not going to answer that, but your Italian is *benissimo*. The MTC knows how to teach languages, don't they?"

She switched to English. "You taught it all to me, Alex, and it got me here. I had only two weeks immersive because I had to switch from Castilian Spanish."

Alex flashed his crooked smile. "I couldn't have taught you so much. You're just smart, Jenn."

"Well, thanks. College is in both our futures, isn't it? Aren't you going to quit your job so you can go, Alex?"

"I don't know, I was supposed to go home in January." He looked away.

"You do still want to be a doctor, don't you?" She knew his desire to study medicine came from the misdiagnosis of his father's deadly cancer three years ago.

"Sure, but first I'm going to work this job for at least a year. I'll be able to pay for college with the money I'm making."

Candles gently illuminated their *tartufo* desserts and the bottom of his face as he sipped his coffee. She told him about 'The Last Judgment' and how much it reminded her of the New Testament she was reading, and how Jesus was even more than she thought he was.

"Have you ever heard Handel's Messiah?" she asked him.

"Once, I think," he answered, preoccupied. Where was the spiritual, happy Alex she once knew?

"I heard the Mormon Tabernacle Choir sing it last Christmas when the whole family went to a performance. Remember the song 'For unto Us a Child is born?' "

"It's from Isaiah, isn't it?"

"Yes. The words say 'he will be called Wonderful Counselor, Mighty God, Everlasting Father, and Prince of Peace.' All those words describe Jesus."

"Right. So what do you want to tell me?"

His attitude was wrong. She backed down, deflated. "Nothing. It's a beautiful song . . . about who Jesus is, that's all." How could Alex take those words for granted? She'd wanted him to validate what she learned they truly meant. That's why he's different, she thought. What if Alex was losing his once strong faith? The thought made her feel cold inside.

"Hey, what time do you have? I miss my phone, but I'm getting it tomorrow." Alex picked at his lavish dessert with a spoon.

"Time doesn't matter, does it? I'm past curfew anyway."

"I always got you home in time, didn't I?"

"You did, even after prom."

"I remember; your dad made sure of it. Jenn, I still feel bad about what happened to you at prom."

She hesitated. "Did I ever thank you for saving me from Bridger? I owe you big time."

Alex shook his head. "You don't owe me; I kind of liked punching him in the nose. I have wondered about something, though."

"What?"

"How did he get you downstairs with him?"

She took a long breath. "When I came out of the ladies room I thought you'd be there. You said you'd meet me on the first level of the Capitol.

Well, Bridger was there instead. Maybe he'd been in the men's room. I don't know. . ."

"Or that predator followed you." Alex frowned. "I took too long talking to Tony upstairs; it was my fault."

"No, you got there at the right time. I shouldn't have trusted him. He told me he'd show me a shortcut to the Hall of Governors, and since his dad was running for State Senator, he had special access. I don't know why I followed; I knew I shouldn't have been alone with him. He sounded respectful, and said it would only take a minute. But once he got me in the dark hall, he grabbed me before I could run . . ."

"That phony jerk! It makes me so mad I could spit. But why on earth would you want to see the Hall of Governors?"

"He lied about a new picture of my grandfather, Brigham Young. I hadn't been there since I was a kid so I believed him. Too curious, I guess."

"Oh well, Jenn, it's all past now. But it's going to take a while for me to forgive myself." His dessert was only half eaten.

She took a spoon and got a bite from his plate. "Because you came, he didn't do much more than tear my dress. But I had to grow up through it. Life got serious because . . . that night I felt closer to you than I ever have. Love is serious, and we have to be careful not to hurt each other."

His eyebrows crossed. "What do you mean? Are you about to hurt me?"

"I would never hurt you if I could help it."

"Sounds like you're breaking it off with me."

"No, Alex. I don't want to break up with you."

His voice intensified. "You know I'm afraid of losing you, Jenn."

He paid the tab, and they walked out to the piazza where the lights brightened the cool air and the atmosphere was like some dream. Remembering a year ago when they'd walked under the Christmas Temple Square lights, she thought she was such a different person now, more open and mature and she knew this young man truly loved her. Even if her family disapproved of him, they were wrong. Surely they would grow to love him if . . . they'd only take time to understand him.

"You're shivering," he said. He put his arm around her in the chilly night air and led her to a kiosk in the piazza. "This one?" he asked, holding up a sky blue pashmina shawl. She nodded, and he paid for it, not balking at the expensive price.

"Tonight I had to buy one just for you; one that matches your eyes."

Wrapped in luxurious softness, she felt warm again. Everything felt so comfortable with Alex next to her. It was the first time Jennalee felt free to be herself, her true self, in months. How she'd missed this sense of rightness and togetherness.

"Jenn, you're getting farther from me. No matter how hard I try, I can't convince you to be with me." Alex's shoulders drooped.

"I only want to be where you are."

"Do you?" he shot back.

She took his hand and held it, and they continued to walk, coming upon an outside dance area where globe lights in rainbow colors hung, with soft music played by a lone guitarist.

She squeezed his hand. "Let's dance, Alex. Just a sec, I'll kick these clunkers off. If I remember right, you won't step on my toes."

He seemed happier. "Tony isn't here with his iPod and our song," he said, "so I'll sing it."

Their song at prom was 'I Will Be Here'. She'd thought about it afterwards whenever she missed Alex because the song described a forever loyalty, a lasting love. They danced and Alex sang it, half whispering into her ear. She closed her eyes. At the end his voice broke.

She couldn't bear to hear his sadness. "Alex, we'll be okay."

He kept singing, but cut off again. "That's all I can do. I don't see how Steven Curtis Chapman can sing it all the way through. It's too sad because . . . you *won't* be here."

His hopelessness, after a soul-stirring day at the Vatican touched her to the core. "Alex, you're in some kind of trouble, aren't you?"

He didn't answer but took her hand and kissing it, walked her off the tiny dance floor. He entwined his fingers with hers as they walked away from the music.

"I want to be here for you, Jenn, but what about you? Can you be here for me?" He gazed at her directly. "Is it too much for me to ask?"

The light around his hair formed a bluish aura under the Italian moon. He reached into his jacket pocket and took out a glittering ring. She knew it was perfect for her as soon as she saw it, with its large diamond in the center of deep red rubies. But the realization he was proposing hit her. Not yet, Alex, not now. She couldn't take it.

"I love you. I want to marry you, Jenn, as soon as we can."

"As soon as we can . . . ?"

"Like, now. Afterwards, we can live in the villa with Nonna and my uncle. We can live in the unused wing of the house." He took her hand, and slipped the ring on her finger. It fit, and she looked at it in shock. They'd barely reunited, and Alex was pushing too fast. Hot tears pooled in her eyes.

"Jenn," he said, "you're not supposed to cry."

"Alex, I need time . . ." What was he thinking? This proposal was all wrong, but the ring glittered in the night air as if forcing her to say 'yes'.

He waited with her there, silent in the piazza until she found her voice.

"This was your *real* surprise, wasn't it? Not just the motorbike ride around Rome."

He nodded, his eyebrows high in concern. "Jenn, I wanted this to be special. I was sure you'd say 'yes'."

"I can't say 'yes'; not now."

"The ring's my pledge to you that I love you. My grandmother gave it to me to give to you. Don't you like it?"

"It's the most beautiful ring ever . . . and I love you, too, I just . . ." The dam broke and tears began to pour. She choked down sobs. Alex stepped back.

"If we're married, Jenn, everything will work out."

"That . . . is . . . not . . . true and you know it."

She shivered even in the shawl and he took off his jacket and put it around her. "You're cold. C'mon, I'll take you home on the scooter."

The ring on her finger felt heavy. Nothing had been decided that night. Alex parked a block away from her room on the Via Margutta. They took off their helmets in silence. There was no talk until they stopped under a street-light across from the apartment. He took her hands again and they faced each other. Golden shafts of light shining on his head made him appear to be a Fra Angelico angel. She loved him. But, in reality, how could she *ever* marry him?

"Jenn, you have my ring, but you didn't say 'yes'."

"I want to say 'yes', Alex, but everything is so confusing. I know what you want me to do, but it's hard."

"I thought you'd say 'yes' right away and that would be it. Now we're back to living a lie."

"Alex," she said, "you have to wait for me. You jumped ahead. Here, I'll give it back to you."

"No, Jenn. Put it around your neck with the cross . . . I wasn't trying to force you."

"Yes, you were. You were at least trying to force everything to be perfect, Alex, and it can't be. Not with us."

"So my timing isn't right? Okay, keep it until you can give me an answer."

She nodded, got out her silver chain, and slipped the ring on it. Another secret to hide near her heart under her clothes.

"Alex, we're meeting on the Spanish steps tomorrow, aren't we?" she asked. "I can give you an answer tomorrow."

"Listen, Jenn, we can't stay like this forever. We're between worlds. My world tips one way and yours is the other way, over there with Sister Sweet and Sour."

"I know you're disappointed but if you can wait for tomorrow . . ."

He let go of her hands. "They've won, haven't they? You want to be Sister Young representing the LDS Church, not my fiancée."

"It's too fast for me, Alex. Too complicated."

"A missionary who doesn't even believe what she's telling people."

"Wait a minute, that's not fair. How do you know how I feel? I believe most of it . . . but you're right, I am confused on a few things."

His anger roared back in the dark predawn. "Let me help your confusion by putting it like this. Your choice needs to be me or the Church."

"Please, Alex . . ." she stumbled.

"I'll try to forget you, because I see we don't have a chance. I knew they'd win. I knew it," he said shaking his head, his face in agony.

A sharp voice erupted from her. "Wait a minute. Listen, you weren't around when I needed you. You were driving a Maserati in a fancy suit, taking clients to lunch. What about your part in all this? Would you give up your high paying job for me? You're the one living a lie."

He pulled back, tense. "What do you mean?"

"What about *my* feelings? You and I should decide these things together at the right time. I have to know with all my being that I can count on you because I won't have a family if I marry you. I'll lose everything in my life if I say 'yes'."

"Lose everything? I know your parents don't like me, but it won't be that bad."

"Yes, it will. My parents will be devastated and will tell my brothers to shun me. And there will be no going back. I could leave if I could totally trust you. But right now, you're acting secretive and not worthy of my trust. We need to wait."

"Okay," he said, "so we should discuss things, Jenn."

"I'm not sure about you. How do I know that a *Signorina* isn't waiting in the wings to adore the man you've become?"

Did a guilty look pass before his eyes? "What do you mean, the man I've become?"

"So different than the guy I fell for last year. Money has gone to your head."

Alex stepped further away from her. "Easy for you to say, rich all your life, your parents setting you up to marry a guy with piles of cash. You never had to worry about anything, Jennalee, especially money."

She tried not to show her hurt. "Alex, I was attracted to you because you *weren't* about money. I was free to be myself with you. There were no lies between us; you had no agenda for my life. That's what made me love you, because you didn't care about stepping on people to get to the top, you didn't care about money or your image. You were happier then."

"So maybe my life *is* different now. I have to keep up an image because. . ."

"Back then, you were more like Jesus than anybody else I'd ever known and I loved that about you. Now you're distant from him. If you'd offered me the ring then, I would've said 'yes', but now . . . you've changed too much."

"Jenn, I'm still the same. It's just this job . . ."

"I think you're losing your faith."

He stared at her, his eyes round. She whirled around and crossed the street toward her room in the apartment building.

"Wait, Jennalee," he said, following her to the vine-covered entrance. "I'm sorry . . . you do need more time. Tomorrow night, we'll decide all this." His face was sad. She watched him go all the way down the street to where he'd left the scooter, his shoulders drooped and defeated.

Trying to hush her own sobs against her fist, she unlocked the door and stood in the foyer, shaking. Jennalee missed the tight, loving hug that was his way of saying goodbye. This time she'd hurt him bad. She felt like running out to the dark street but knew he was gone.

He was right, she was stuck in a lie, and it had grown until a chasm opened between them. Tiptoeing, she let herself back into the room, crawled into bed and choked her sobs down. Her roommate slept on, or at least Jennalee thought so.

17

THE TRIALS OF AMMON

When Brent parked his BMW in front of the old lap-sided house in Price, Ammon's sisters were waiting for them. With Otto in the hospital, at least the family was pushing to have a normal celebration for Ammon. The three girls cheered, waving like football fans while holding a sign that read, "Welcome Home Elder Carr."

"They're extremely proud of you," said Brent.

"Wow, they're so much taller. Tricia's fifteen and in high school. I can't believe it. Look at Bethany and Jewel."

"How old are they?"

"Beth's thirteen and Jewel's eleven. So tall."

Tall and half-starved, thought Brent. Must be a family trait to have toothpick limbs because Ammon did, too.

They hurried out of the car as his mom exited the house, untying an apron protecting her Sunday best clothes. Brent could see she'd been pretty in her younger days but was now faded and worn, with wispy blondish hair around her face and dark circles under her eyes.

With four women, he knew it would take a while for hugs and tears to subside. Brent stood on one foot, rubbing his new casual shoes on the back of his jeans. They were dusty from the rest stop on Soldier Summit.

Ammon loosened the many arms on him and introduced his friend. The girls eyed him, cautious, but Mrs. Carr nodded and shook hands with a damp palm, holding her apron.

"We prayed every day for both of you and now you're home. But things have taken a bad turn here." She broke down sobbing as her only son held her under the weeping willow tree in their front yard.

At last, Ammon escorted her into the house. Brent held the door for the three girls before following them inside where a long dining table held a roasted turkey on a platter. There was a steaming mound of mashed potatoes and a deep pitcher of gravy. Blue crepe paper and red balloons were tied to the light fixture above plates of corn on the cob and warm rolls with jam in individual bowls.

Ammon's mom had cooked a huge welcome home meal in spite of the severe crisis the family was under. He tried to relieve the sadness a little.

"Mrs. Carr, you don't know how we dreamed of a feast like this in Argentina, remember, Ammon?"

His friend nodded. "Thanks, Mom," he said in a voice so quiet the ticking of the clock covered it.

Brent could see the Carrs weren't at all rich and tried to keep their furniture new-looking with covers and doilies. But in spite of the effort, everything in the house was as faded and worn as Mrs. Carr herself. At his own house, his mother renewed the furnishings every year or two.

Slipping into his family's leadership role, Ammon carved the turkey with a chef's knife as the three girls openly stared at Brent, unable to hide shy smiles. Watching Ammon made him wonder if his friend had often acted as the man of the house because of Otto's shift work in the mine and gambling forays to Nevada. Seemed so.

"I've told your father you were coming home," said Mrs. Carr. "He doesn't respond, but I know he heard me. He'll wake up soon. Won't he, girls?"

The sisters appeared troubled at the mention of their dad. Shock from their father's coma weighed heavy on Ammon, too. Brent could see it in his slumped shoulders and worry lines. He resolved to help his friend as much as he could.

While Brent devoured the enormous meal, Ammon left most of his food on his plate.

"Leave the dishes, we'll just put the left-overs away and then go." Mrs. Carr waved her hands at Brent as he poured soap into the sink. "We need to take Ammon up to the hospital to see Dad right away."

While two of the girls rode with their mom, the oldest, Tricia, climbed into the back seat of the BMW. In the passenger seat, Ammon's hands formed claws as they got closer to the hospital.

"Don't be nervous. Dad doesn't look too bad," Trish told him.

"What happened? I mean for real? Was he drunk?"

"No, nothing like that. Everyone said it was an accident."

"You don't have to stick up for him."

"Ammon, don't be so negative. It wasn't Dad's fault. He fell into moving machinery."

Empty parking lots surrounded Price's too-large hospital and Brent got in close to the entrance. He was impressed with the well-designed building, but the staff wasn't too friendly.

Hospital nurses passed them without eye contact as they made their way to Room 205 where a pale man lay plugged into an IV for sustenance.

His eyes were closed, his breathing shallow. Dark hair clung to his balding head, wet with sweat. Otto Carr lay between the world of the living and the dead. To Brent, he didn't look good.

Ammon took his father's hand and stood next to the bed railing. Brent hated to see his friend like this. Things were hard for them in Argentina but now Ammon's entire future was at stake. He wouldn't be able to go back to college, and might be poor all his life.

Brent offered to stay with Otto while the entire family stepped into the hallway to talk to the doctors. After sitting there in the quiet for ten minutes, he remembered Ammon's mom had said her husband could hear every word.

"Mr. Carr, I'm your son's friend; we were in Argentina together." Was it his imagination or did the patient's breathing change?

He glanced at his buzzing phone. Rachel's text asked how he was, told him she prayed for him constantly. He spoke his answer into the phone and the text was sent.

> You don't know how much your prayers help. Thanks. Can you pray for a man named Otto? Ammon's father. He's in a coma and I'm with him now. Let's pray he wakes up.

Her answer was swift.

> I will pray as you pray and I believe it will be done.

It gave him courage, that text. He spoke again to Otto, this time about Rachel and Alison, and good times in Argentina. Brent even told him about Jesus.

"I think Ammon likes Alison. Me, I definitely feel something for Rachel. And she's praying for you right now, so I will, too." Otto's cheeks were a tinge less pale. Brent took the same limp hand Ammon had held. The man didn't answer, but his throat made a tiny sound.

He prayed for several minutes in a strong loud voice, but later only remembered the last part: "Jesus, you care about this family, and I know you can heal Otto of all his injuries. I ask you to heal him so he can wake up. Then you can show him your truth in the all-powerful name of Jesus Christ. Amen."

Brent sat down, a flush coming over his face. He'd never prayed like that before, even in his mind. Where had the words come from? He stared at the now reddish face on the bed.

Otto's eyes blinked open, closed for a second then opened again. Brent didn't know what to do. He rushed to the door and called out, but no one was there. He spun back into the room and pressed the nurse's button.

By now, Otto Carr was wide awake, straining to lift his head off the pillow.

"It's OK, Mr. Carr. Your family will be right back. I'm Brent, who went with Ammon to Argentina."

Otto blinked hard over and over. His mouth moved and his unused weak voice tried to communicate.

"You . . . told me. . . Ammon . . ."

"He'll be right back."

"Tell Ammon . . . it . . . was no accident." He was clear.

"What, Mr. Carr? Did you say it wasn't an accident? Your head injury?"

A cloud passed over Otto's stark blue eyes. He looked from side to side, his neck straining off the pillow. "You're not one of them, are you?" His voice croaked.

"I'm your son's friend."

Otto relaxed on the pillow again. "He'll believe me."

Frustrated, Brent called again for a nurse. No one came.

"Now rest, Mr. Carr, and I'll go get the nurse. They'll be excited you're awake."

The man rasped, "Wait. They pushed me. Hear?"

"I hear you, sir."

"Tried to jump clear, but they . . . want me dead."

"Mr. Carr, I can ask the police to investigate."

"No police. No, no, they're all in it together. I can only tell *you*, son."

Rachel's text came through as Brent covered up the quivering man with a flannel sheet.

So how's Otto?

He woke up! Brent answered.

Glory! She typed back. Rachel got results from prayer, he thought, something he hadn't been accustomed to in his other life.

18

'OUT OF THE WRECK I RISE'

Alex tried to think of a way out. He dreaded the drive to Abruzzo to pick up the Putifaro contract and his cell phone, but the day came. Every time he drummed up courage to tell his uncle the whole story, he couldn't get it out. Now he had to go by himself. Alex reasoned that Largo Putifaro couldn't have believed his wife, so everything should be okay, shouldn't it?

Italy's superhighways are made for speed, so before Alex exited on to country roads, he opened up and went fast. Those fifty miles east of Rome went by in a flash. The Maserati could reach175 mph if he wanted it to, but Alex wouldn't risk his uncle's prized possession. Still, the car's abilities were a temptation to take it to the limit.

After being with Jennalee the last two nights, Alex couldn't focus. The proposal had ended in disaster and he didn't know why. Even though she cared about him, it wasn't enough for her to leave her mission. Jennalee didn't want to be rescued; she intended to stay where she was. He had to move on and he was angry enough to do it.

He'd find someone else . . . like Firenza. He turned up the music to dull his thoughts. A future working in Italy might not be so bad . . . working until he had the lifestyle he wanted. He could buy his own sports car. Maybe a Lamborghini.

But how could he forget her? She was as beautiful as ever and there was no denying God intervened to get them together, yet Alex was utterly unhappy. Could he wait seventeen months while the Church held her? No, he'd lose her in that time. Too much could happen and may have already happened. Bridger obviously waited for her in Utah.

No . . . it was not the life he wanted. He wanted to live in the now. Tonight would be a crucial point, the final decision in their relationship. Maybe she'd show up on the Spanish steps with a suitcase and free herself.

"God, whatever it takes!" was his reckless prayer thrown up to heaven. Then, he tuned in to a Sirius rock music radio station on the state-of-the-art sound system in the Ghibli. Prayer was forgotten and he drove faster. A lot faster.

Alex almost missed his exit off the superhighway, screeching the brakes to make the ramp. Leaving scrub oak behind, the mountain road wound through the green hills of Abruzzo. He checked the time; he'd be at the Putifaro vineyard and winery in half an hour. The best wine in Italy made from Montepulciano grapes awaited him. His sommelier's nose began to pick up scents of each of the micro regions he passed.

Simple. With the important signed contract in hand, he'd drive back to meet Jennalee at the Spanish Steps late that night. She'd say yes and leave, he knew she would. If she didn't want to marry right away, he'd tell her they'd wait. But he wanted to be with her, either in Italy or in Utah.

Rain sprinkled his windshield, changing to bigger drops, then large flakes of snow. He set the wipers on low speed, but switched to high as the frozen mix intensified. Water ran in rivulets across sections of the pavement.

He slowed the car, took off his sunglasses, and set them on the passenger seat. If only he had his cell phone, he could call and tell them he may be late. Hemmed in by a rocky mountain on one side, a steep drop-off on the other, he steered around a sharp curve. Sudden blurred red lights appeared in front of him. Alex hit the brakes and hoped for the best.

Jesus help me! The Maserati swerved sideways and stopped inches from the back of what turned out to be a heavy truck. The slow motion movie in his wind shield dazed him as he got out, his door so close to the back of a delivery truck it barely opened.

The driver waved his arms from the side of the pavement, white with wet snow. Nobody could see his car around the curve, so Alex scrambled over a short stone wall between the road and the mountainside. Sure enough, the next car rounded the curve too fast, and he saw a woman's face, a look of surprise, and then heard the terrible squeal of brakes hit too late.

Smashed at such a speed, the Maserati threw crunched pieces of blue metal around him as he ducked down. The sound of bending metal and breaking glass deafened him, and he put his hands on his ears. Smoke from burning rubber filled his nose along with the smell of spilled gasoline.

Was it his heart he heard or the thump, thump of his Maserati rolling sideways down the cliff? The deafening impact echoed in the air as he looked up to see his car gone. The woman's vehicle was on fire, and he leaped over the wall to help her. His peripheral vision caught the truck driver coming to help, too.

She slumped over the airbag, blood pouring from a gash on her head, but she was alive. He tried the door handle and it opened, crookedly held by its hinges. The injured woman moaned in pain, her head lying on the white airbag.

"Call an ambulance, *pronto*!" Alex barked to the truck driver, who held a cell phone.

Then, to the woman, he asked in clear Italian, "Can you move? What hurts?"

"My ribs," she said, breathless, "and my legs."

"I must lift you out of the car," he said, "I'll be gentle."

"No! I don't want to move," she screamed.

Alex didn't hesitate; he put one hand under her seat and the other around her back. She instinctively held on to his neck, groaning the whole time. He slid her out as fire covered the front end of the car. The only safe area to go was back over the half-wall, now covered with snow, and he took her there. Somebody doused the car fire with an extinguisher.

"Help is on the way. I'll stay with you," Alex said in a soothing way as he laid her on the grass. He took off his jacket and put it over her. He thought she probably had broken bones. He stayed with the injured woman until the truck driver, who was called Marco, found a doctor among the other drivers. Only then did he leave her.

Alex couldn't bear to see where his Maserati had been smashed. Pieces of blue mica-flecked metal littered the slushy pavement. Flakes of snow melted on his face and soaked his shirt as he stared numbly down the cliff at his uncle's once-magnificent car. He'd been seconds away from being inside as it rolled over the cliff.

He'd lost the laptop and his briefcase, but found his sunglasses on the pavement, without a scratch on them. Putting them inside his shirt, he decided to see what caused the traffic stop in the first place. He walked around the curve, where a Ferrari sports car was stopped in front of a road block of huge concrete barriers. Someone would've had to use heavy equipment to position them.

The baffled driver of the car stood, shaking his head near it. Alex went over to him. "Is this an official roadblock? Did I miss a sign?"

"There was no warning. On a blind curve, too." The man looked wealthy, with a tailored suit and top-of-the-line shoes, though both were now soaked.

"At least your car's okay, mine was hit . . . it rolled over the side of the mountain." Alex put his shirt collar up against the cold wind and the man took him by the arm.

"I heard the crash. I'm sorry, but here now . . . we have worse trouble."

Heavy brush on the side of the mountain moved, and four masked men holding automatic weapons came into view. Bewildered, Alex and the other man were told to put their hands up. This can't be real, he thought. Then a very solid gun nudged him in the back.

19

TEMPLES WHO WALK

That day Jennalee and Terrilyn found themselves on bus 118 riding to the ancient catacombs on the Via Appia Antica. They wanted to go early to see the catacombs the elders had recommended and then to dinner at an LDS member's apartment.

Jennalee gazed out the bus window, unsettled about Alex and their angry words last night. If he really loved her, he'd wait for her. Alex had no idea what kind of extreme act it would be to leave her mission and how she'd be reprimanded. But she had to decide by tonight when they met . . . one more time.

Jennalee glanced down at her faithful but ugly walking shoes from Provo Mall, now grateful to have them. Between walking and riding buses, it had taken the better part of an hour to reach the catacombs of San Sebastiano. The old Appian Way was the main artery of ancient Rome, stretching for miles with signs of a civilization from over two thousand years ago. Joggers and bicyclists rode over the stone road, apparently ignoring the sheer age of it all.

When they reached the church holding the catacombs, she stopped in front of a long glass-covered compartment. Inside was a white marble statue of the martyr St. Sebastian, shot by arrows and gracefully rendered in a dying pose. Clean indeed, for martyrdom. Still, she thought, he'd died to follow Jesus and a gentle statue to commemorate him was appropriate.

A crowd gathered in the foyer of the church to go down into the crypts. The girls sidled towards the English speaking tour guide: a tiny man, with sparkling eyes and a ready smile. He took in their LDS name badges and held up his hand, indicating they could join his tour. Guess this place didn't require they remove the nametags.

"Welcome. This way, please," said the pleasant little man. "You must keep up! Do not dilly-dally; eleven kilometers of tufa rock tunnels are before us and people have been known to disappear." He smiled an elfish grin as Terrilyn rolled her eyes.

They descended into a damp hallway and Jennalee shuddered with sudden cold. The tunnel was carved rock from floor to ceiling, with niches cut out from the side walls. Far from macabre, it was a holy place, memorializing lives well lived and deaths well died, sacred in its very echoes.

Serious now, the guide said, "Early Christians were targeted by the government. Their allegiance was not Roman enough. They were hated because they opposed a way of life based on hedonism and pleasure."

"Mormons are persecuted, too," whispered Terrilyn, "because we don't go along with the culture."

"But we don't have to bury our dead in secret tunnels."

"We were chased and hounded until we reached Utah, and even today . . ."

"Shh," Jennalee said, "listen."

The historian's eyes caught Jennalee's. He looked through her very soul; in a kind way, she thought later, but still . . . right through to the core of her being. They entered a circular room lined with niches.

"Try a cubicle out for size," said the guide. She knew most of the people laughed from discomfort and she was uncomfortable too. Who would want to crawl into a tomb?

"Not much room, I'm afraid. The niches are tight; many of you wouldn't fit." The man gave a hearty laugh then said, "Don't miss the richness of early Christian symbols and drawings on the walls."

Jennalee spotted one of these; the faded reddish paint showed a simple figure of an unbearded man in robes with hands held high. She pointed it out to Terrilyn, who said, "Who cares? I'm grossed out in here. Who does he think he is, that little man?"

Wow, thought Jennalee, confronting mortality wasn't Sister Sweet and Sour's strong suit. In a wider space of the tunnel, she recognized some Greek letters inside a fish design just as the tour man approached them. It was the fish on Alex's notebook in high school.

"Young lady, you are seeing an ICHTHUS, the ancient Greek word for fish. The letters themselves are an acronym for Jesus, Son of God, Savior. It stands as a secret code among early Christians to avoid enemies wanting to kill them. One Christ follower would walk up to another and draw an arc in the dirt, like this." He bent down and traced an arc on the stone floor with his finger.

"If the other was a true believer, they would complete the fish by drawing the other arc. No verbal communication needed. Go ahead, my dear, trace the other half of the fish."

Jennalee, temples beating wildly, crouched down and finished the invisible fish with a trembling finger. How could this man know she was secretly thinking about becoming a true Christ-follower? She hoped Terrilyn hadn't noticed anything amiss in her face. The tour guide smiled directly at her, "You see? With this simple act, both knew they were believers."

The air stagnated in the tunnel as the man continued to talk. "Christians refused to worship the Roman emperor and idols in the temples. They were accused of disloyalty, atheism, and hatred towards mankind. Often they were held responsible for fires, plagues and floods. Who among you hasn't heard of the Emperor Nero blaming Christians for a fire he set himself?"

Several people on the tour nodded.

"As dangerous enemies of Rome, Christians were torn by wild animals, crucified, stabbed, or put on the rack to die."

The tourists followed their guide upstairs on their way out of the catacombs, back to the foyer to stand under paintings of early saints. The guide's eyes glittered. "The Romans tried to stop it, but Christianity spread like the wind. For the first time in history, they had a promise of eternal life for believing in Jesus, and even females and children were included. This was more than the old Roman gods offered."

He coughed. "Today, millions call themselves Christians. Are *they* willing to live and die for Jesus? I'll let you answer the question yourselves." He inclined his head. "Other gods require temples, but Jesus set up Christ-followers to actually *become* temples of his Holy Spirit. We are temples with legs . . . temples who walk wherever he tells us to go."

Temples who walk? Jennalee studied him as he stood stock still and said, "Thank you for viewing this splendid place of joyful persecution where the first Christians overcame death through the resurrection power of Jesus." He took a funny bow and as the group dispersed, he disappeared into an office.

Once they were outside in the sunny plaza in front of the church, Terrilyn said, "It was so stuffy down there, I could barely breathe. And that little man was crazy, absolutely bonkers."

"He knew a lot of Christian history. . ." said Jennalee, enjoying the sight of umbrella pine trees, their canopies unmoving against the soft light of the Roman sky. She felt elated to be alive after coming out of the crypt but she'd be mocked if she revealed her real thoughts.

"Sister Young, I don't see why we're here looking at all this stuff. Our scriptures are more reliable and our temples more splendid. What did he mean by saying a bunch of burial niches were splendid? And everyone knows a temple is a building."

Jennalee swallowed hard. "But we believe in the Holy Spirit inside of us, don't we? He did say strange things, but he was sincere about what he said."

"Our gospel will win out in the end because it's based on the Prophet Joseph Smith's revelations. These people are steeped in old saints and superstitions."

Jennalee pulled at the irritating garment under her skirt and Terrilyn glared at her. "The corruption of the Bible came *after* these early Christians, you know," said Jennalee. "Our Church recognizes early Christian martyrs, too."

"Where are you going with this, Sister Young? You're in dangerous water. I know what you're thinking; you think that crazy guy is right."

"I think what they believed is so very different than what we believe. They didn't have the ordinances of the temple, for instance. Don't you see? Our Church claims to have restored what Jesus intended before the corruption of the Middle Ages. So it should match the early Christians very closely. But it doesn't."

"You're overthinking. Of course they believed differently. We have the restored gospel, a better one. They didn't have anything. They only had bits and pieces of the New Testament, which may have been corrupted even then."

"So what made it possible for them to give their lives for Christ? They were martyred in terrible ways, while asking God to forgive the people who killed them. They were assured of eternal life without doing anything but believing in Jesus . . . wow."

"Wait a minute. We give hope to people, too, hope of working for perfection towards Celestial Heaven. Hope to live a good life, marry, and have forever families. What could be better? Did anyone ever tell you that you think too much, Sister Young?"

"You just did. Twice." It *wasn't* hope; it was a set of rules.

Their steps dragged as the girls walked along the Appian Way until the junction of Via della Sette Chiesi, the Street of Seven Churches. "We go this way," said Jennalee.

"Oh my heck, we're two kilometers from Sister Agosta's apartment, and I have a blister from my shoe," Terrilyn whined.

"Trade you shoes; what size do you wear?"

No trade was possible; the offending shoes were two sizes bigger than Jennalee's. Terrilyn limped for a slow fifteen minutes. "How much further?"

Jennalee answered, "Let's rest up here." A tattered sign behind overgrown shrubbery announced the entrance to the Domitilla Catacombs.

Her companion groaned. "Not another ancient burial ground! Well, maybe they have a Band-Aid. On top of this, I have to go to the bathroom."

Jennalee tried the door in the graffiti-plastered wall. Locked. She wiggled the handle but no one heard. "Stay here," said Jennalee, sprinting to an ornate iron gate where a bent-over old nun jangled keys.

The nun had kind eyes, read her badge and nodded. In Italian, she said, "We're closed now. You are welcome to return tomorrow."

"*Per favore*, do you have a bandage for my friend's foot?"

"*Sì*," she said, asking more questions. Jennalee explained as the nun observed Terrilyn limping through the parking lot to where they stood. "Tsk, tsk, poor girl," she said, and unlocked the gate. Terrilyn handed her backpack to Jennalee, who felt four empty water bottles inside.

The old nun indicated for Terrilyn to follow her. Jennalee helped her companion to a little closet where she sat in a chair until the nun emerged from another room with first aid supplies. "I'll wait for you outside," Jennalee said, "I feel awkward in this tiny room."

"Okay," said Terrilyn, frowning with disapproval, "I'll watch our backpacks."

Glad to be free of her companion, Jennalee wandered in the courtyard swirling with lush vines outside the catacomb. In the back of her mind was the pointed question Alex would ask her that night. Could she leave her mission?

She was alone with her thoughts as she walked up the swept earthen path and the air stilled like the eye of a storm. Under a gnarled olive tree, she bent down and traced the bottom arc of an ICHTHUS fish for the second time that day.

"I'm so confused," she said aloud. She thought she knew who Jesus was but she realized her knowledge of him was through the lens of the LDS Church. When she'd met Alex, a new Jesus opened up to her.

"I can't fix all this," she said to the vines clinging to the stucco wall. She missed Utah and the familiar comfort of her childhood faith; it felt secure to belong to a righteous group of people and too scary to lose it all. She shouldn't question it. Doubt was sin and that was that.

Didn't Jesus have to achieve eternal progression to become a god? And she would be a goddess in Celestial Heaven if she followed the same tenets: obedience and faith, marriage to an LDS man. Jesus was married, too, wasn't he? The LDS genealogies proved it in the records, in black and white.

Confusion riled her. The New Testament never mentioned any of this and Jesus himself said there was no marriage in heaven. His words were in black and white, too. She glanced towards the church door. Terrilyn was taking a long time, giving her a chance to wrestle with these questions before she saw Alex.

It couldn't be right what Alex said, that faith alone justifies you. Then again, the martyrs believed it. No, the atonement of Jesus was done so she could work out her individual salvation through the ordinances of the Church. What about the warm burning feeling in her heart when she gave her memorized testimony at age thirteen to her local ward? Was it only the emotion of the moment or was it proof Mormonism was really true? Everyone she knew believed only in warm tingly proof.

What had she just seen in the New Testament in Ephesians? *"For it is by grace you have been saved, through faith—and this is not from yourselves, it is the gift of God— not by works, so that no one can boast."* Faith first, then grace, then salvation. No works.

She shook her head as if to clear it. How could she ever question the Church of Jesus Christ of Latter-day Saints, the Prophet Joseph Smith, Council of the Twelve Apostles, the Quorum of Seventy and General Authorities? And millions of members besides? She felt small as an ant like she had at St. Peter's, only this time she was an ant smashed on the floor of the Salt Lake Temple.

She had a terrible thought her LDS faith wasn't quite right, that what happened in the temple was actually wrong. But she couldn't tell anybody.

Then a still small voice inside her mind said, "Ask me."

She knew that voice, a shepherd's voice, risen from the New Testament. It was Jesus.

"Okay," she said, "are you the Everlasting Father in Isaiah? I don't understand. Are you a Spirit and not flesh and bone? Can I know you like Alex says?"

The air was powerfully still. Nothing. Jennalee was determined as tears rolled. "Can you see me?" Her soul hurt. "Jesus, are you really there? Do you love me?" And before those words were out, her questions were answered.

A warm wind surrounded her full force, embracing her in a divine hug. Heat poured from her head to her toes, bathing her in the most tender love she'd ever felt. A vat of warm oil was poured over her head and there were no doubts now. The presence of Jesus was all around her. This was beyond any man's words. There was no 'burning in the bosom'; this had nothing to do with her or her emotions. Tears dried on her face as clarity replaced confusion.

She whirled around in the dissipating wind, her arms spread wide and high, like the faded figure painted on the catacomb wall. He'd shown her that he was real, that he loved her, and heard her. The wind . . . which actually wasn't wind, retreated, leaving the air as calm as it had been earlier. Jennalee glowed with a fourth dimension fire and she hoped it would never go out. The miracle of Jesus 'hugging' her lasted two seconds, but left her with a completely new life.

A heavy church door clanged shut. "Sister Young? Are you out here?"

Jennalee crouched under the olive tree and drew the top arc of the ICHTHUS fish. Breathing gratitude, she knew she was born-again in spirit and truth. It's complete; *I'm all in and it's because of Jesus and his love for me.*

She jerked back into her world and saw Terrilyn McKay striding towards her, an odd look on her face. So she stepped away from the tree, leaving the fish symbol in the dust. ICTHUS was engraved in her soul. And Alex . . . she knew how to answer him tonight.

"There you are, Sister Young. Sorry I took so long, but would you believe the nun *washed* my feet? Even with arthritis, she got soft towels and helped me. The blister popped and see the bandage she put on? Isn't it great? And she prayed for me. I . . . couldn't believe it. She even filled our water bottles with ice cold water." She paused. "This was a good place to stop."

Jennalee nodded. "The best stop ever. You're not limping anymore, and neither am I; I can walk straight from now on." She linked arms with the puzzled Terrilyn and marched out on to the sidewalk, strong in loving her life, the world, and yes . . . even her companion.

20

CAMORRA

"Empty your pockets," said a gruff voice next to Alex's ear. The man spoke through a balaclava mask in Italy's Southern dialect.

This could be bad. Alex turned his pockets inside out and spilled the contents on the ground, moving slowly so as not to get shot. His wallet with his cards and money were scooped up by the thieves.

Armed men in black painted faces and dark clothes got out of a car bringing Marco, the truck driver. No other people came from the scene of the wreck. No police, no help. They had captured him, Marco and the rich guy with the Ferrari.

Without looking at the man next to him, Alex whispered, "Mafia?" He felt, rather than saw, his quick, fearful nod. This had to be the Abruzzo mafia known as Camorra he'd heard about.

"Where is your phone?" asked one of the men as another guy patted him down.

"I have no phone," he answered, hoping they'd believe him.

"You lost it in your car!" He laughed, and it echoed against the rain, the rock cliff, and Alex's ear drums. It was the kind of laugh he thought Satan would have.

They'll let us go after they rob us, Alex told himself. It frustrated him that the signed contract and his lost phone waited for him at the Putifaro Vineyard and he would have to leave them there. What would he do with no car and no Euros?

A man in a trench coat approached him, wearing a hat and sunglasses. "You!" he shouted at Alex, "I know who you are."

Sure you do, you just stole my wallet. Alex made sure his face showed no expression.

"I am *Signore* Casalesi," said the man, closer to his ear than he liked. "You are Alexander Dante Campanaro, *si? Americano.*"

"*Si, Signore,*" said Alex. He almost asked why the largest mafia family in Abruzzo was interested in him. He was a small fish.

"We have the power here, *Signore* Campanaro," said the man, his voice on a hair string, "we are the Casalesi family. We say who can do business here and who can't. So sorry about your car."

Alex grimaced, wet hair dripping into his eyes. "It wasn't mine."

"No matter, you will come with us. I see you later."

This was bad, really bad.

Signore Casalesi climbed into a black car which moved around the road block and disappeared deeper into Abruzzo. Until then, he hadn't noticed one of the giant concrete blocks had been moved. How? Then he saw a forklift hidden in the bushes. This was planned by these guys.

A white van started up and rolled towards them as the man behind him took both his arms and tied his wrists with a plastic zip tie. He heard it being pulled tight; felt it almost cutting into his skin.

They did the same to the other two prisoners' hands, then blindfolded them all with black bands and pushed them into the van. Alex finally heard sirens at the scene of the wreck behind them as the white van drove away. Too late for any help.

He could hardly breathe as he lay on the floor of the van. There was nothing he could do about the contract and his phone. And what would Jennalee think when he didn't show up? Would he even be alive tonight?

His imagination raced, with thoughts of his uncle and Jennalee discovering he was dead. He shook, maybe from being soaked to the skin in the rain. No, this was what it's like to shake with fear.

And his Mom . . . if she knew what was happening, what would she do? She'd pray, he thought. Maybe she was praying at this moment. He should, too.

Muttering to himself in English, he prayed on the cold wet floor of the van: "Jesus, I know you're with me but I can't feel you here. Help me, you've got to. There is no one else." The fearful racing thoughts dulled, and his exhaustion caused him to fall into a rough sleep.

21

STRONGHOLDS SURRENDER

Repercussions of what happened to Jennalee in the catacomb garden were immediate. Everything in the world was clearer, colors were brand new. People, even strangers, were more loveable. So this is it, she thought, this is what it is to be born-again. She now saw Terrilyn with a feeling of compassion she knew didn't come from herself. Not her old self anyway. She'd stepped into the spiritual realm that was the Kingdom of God. It had little to do with a church, and everything to do with the love of God. She'd never forget His enormous love, not ever.

The mundane things of earth picked at her, but her vision was still before her eyes. Dinner at a third story walk-up apartment was a joy-filled blur in her mind. Under the table, Sister McKay kicked her. "Why are you so happy?" she hissed.

"Don't know," Jennalee mouthed. But she did know. How could her companion understand? Alex would, though . . . she could hardly wait to see him at midnight.

"This garlic sauce is delicious, and the salad's wonderful." Her compliments made *Signora* Agosta, an LDS convert, smile.

"You're so phony," Terrilyn whispered to her as Sister Agosta jumped up to get a pitcher of lemon water and her son dug into his pasta.

"I am?" It didn't offend her. On the way there, Jennalee tried, but couldn't relate her spiritual experience to Terrilyn. Her companion could not grasp the paradigm shift.

Pepe Agosta wasn't nearly as bad as the elders made him out to be although he tried to flirt with older girls like any thirteen year-old. She tried to keep her happiness from showing too much, risking people thinking she was crazy.

Bits of conversation reached her . . . about the temple's opening. Pepe and his mother agreed to go with them to tour it. Inside her spirit groaned. The temple was no longer relevant in her life. With this thought, a monumental change had happened inside her. Big enough to know she could never go back.

On the bus back to Via Margutta, she melted into her seat, satisfied in the warmth of that overpowering love. No longer would she fidget within the confines of the LDS faith. She knew where she stood with God now. A feeling of private joy overwhelmed her, and she'd have to tell another born-again or burst.

Her head laid on the pillow, but she stayed awake knowing Alex waited for her on the Spanish steps. The way they'd split apart the night before hurt them both. But now, grasping this God-love, it would be simpler to leave her mission so they could be together.

While her companion brushed her teeth in the bathroom down the hall, Jennalee got up and packed a backpack. As soon as Terrilyn fell asleep, she rushed to the Spanish Steps where she waited for Alex. One hour, then two. She nursed a coffee from McDonald's, her first one ever, heaped with cream and sugar. Alex never came. The end of the hour crushed all hope of seeing him that night.

Defeated, she walked back to the room on Via Margutta, and put her backpack under her bed. Either something had happened to Alex or he had left her, broken it off. In the darkness of her room, at three thirty in the morning, she grabbed the missionary cell phone and texted his phone, the one he'd told her not to.

Alex, are you okay? I'm going to leave. I love you too much.

Deleting the text so Terrilyn wouldn't trace it, she hoped Alex had his phone again. She lay on top of her covers, keyed up by caffeine, resting her eyes while her mind was on fire.

At breakfast, she saw a knowing look on Terrilyn's face while they ate dry cereal.

Jennalee tried to play sick. "Sister, I have to stay in today, I'm not well."

"Four hours of sleep for the last three nights would get to anyone, Sister Young. How was our handsome investigator last night?" Terrilyn peered over her bowl, grinning.

"How long have you known?"

"I saw you night before last with him, but I haven't reported you, not yet. Disgusting behavior." Her face contorted in a cruel smile.

"Why not?"

"I'm waiting."

"What for? Just press the lever on the guillotine, Terrilyn."

"Don't you care you'll be in big trouble?"

"Not anymore."

"I know one thing. With a companion like you who's out kissing Italians at night, I want a different one. It's up to you. Should I tell the President the truth, or should I say I don't get along with you?"

"We *don't* get along, so that's no lie. And you think you know the real truth but you don't."

Sister McKay looked at her with beady eyes, her head tilted a bit. "What do you mean, I don't know the real truth?"

"You wouldn't understand even if I told you."

"Try me."

"I think not. Go ahead and tell the President what you know, Terrilyn. It's all over for me anyway."

Jennalee's mind was groggy and her cereal was getting soggy. Day after day, to torture her, Terrilyn played the same Tabernacle Choir CD on an old player. "Turn down the music, I think I hear our cell phone."

"It *is* our phone, where is it?"

"I'll get it." Jennalee picked it up off the floor next to her bed. It was a text.

You will never find him, little Signorina.

Shock numbed her. Someone . . . had Alex's cell. Where was he? She sensed the threat of danger to Alex more than to herself. Her throat tight, she deleted it, and said, "Wrong number."

"It's not from any of our investigators, then?"

Jennalee shook her head.

Terrilyn sneered. "I can tell it's from your Italian boyfriend. I may have to tell this to the President. You know the phone is only for Church business."

"Some random text. No big deal." So random, she thought, who could've sent it?

"Give the phone to me."

Jennalee handed it to her with a feigned yawn.

"You're getting in deeper and deeper, Sister Young. I'm going downstairs to pay the rent since you gave me half. When I come back you better be ready to go with me to tell everything to the President." Terrilyn slammed the door.

Jennalee felt a surge of energy and clear thinking. She took a deep breath. *I'm ready to go alright.* She grabbed her daypack. Everything felt right about this decision. Time to jump off the cliff and trust God to catch her as she fell.

Terrilyn's shrill "Stop!" echoed down the street as Jennalee ran away in her sturdy shoes. Scared she'd be caught, she sprinted faster toward Alex's wine shop. Her feet felt light, like she was a child again and nothing could stop her. Sometimes you just have to jump and trust.

The shop was closed. She banged her fists on the green shutter anyway. "*Signore* Giovanini!" she yelled, but no answer. She tried to remember which days Alex had said he'd be there. Where was he? Needing to hide, she waited in a side street, hoping not to draw too much attention to herself.

In an hour, a handsome man in a suit sauntered up to the shop and opened the shutter. She got up from where she sat on the curb and dusted herself off. Alex talked about his uncle often, and this tall man fit the description. Did he know Alex was missing? He was too calm, she decided, watching his unhurried opening of the shop.

She ran across the street and spoke to him in Italian. "*Buongiorno*, my name is Jennalee Young. I'm a friend of your nephew, Alex Campanaro. Do you know where he is?"

He had a cordial manner and smiled, showing a space between his front teeth. "Come in, come in, a friend of Alessandro's is a friend of mine. Tell me why you are here, *Signorina*, and by all means, speak your native English. I will understand."

Jennalee could see Alex in him, and even Gabe. He had the same crooked smile and his calmness helped her.

"*Mamma mia*, aren't you are the girl my son's been looking for? What a beauty you are."

"*Grazie, Signore* Giovanini," she said, feeling shaky, "I think I can trust you."

"Trust? Why do you say that?" He laughed. "Call me Lucio."

"An hour ago, I ran away from my Church mission so please don't tell them where I am. And Alex is . . . in trouble or missing. I know it."

She told him the whole story of the missed rendezvous and the mysterious text. Uncle Lucio quit smiling. "Maybe he went clubbing out on the town. I was not alarmed because when he's in town he stays here, upstairs in the flat."

"Does Alex ever 'go clubbing'?" she asked, peeved just a little. Maybe he wasn't in danger, only hung over some place.

"No . . . unfortunately, the poor boy is too serious for parties. He was supposed to pick up his phone yesterday in Abruzzo. I should have checked on him. Let's see if he's still upstairs."

They climbed the narrow stairway and she was surprised to see a neat bed made up with a duvet and satin pillows. It amazed her how they'd been alone here during the night in the garden, and he'd never tried to get her upstairs. He wouldn't be partying. But what if he was with someone else?

Jennalee tried to make her voice strong. "When I knew him, he wasn't a partier. So you haven't heard from him at all?"

"No and you see his bed has not been slept in," said Uncle Lucio. "But calm yourself, he probably had to stay over in Abruzzo. The weather can be tricky over the passes."

"But wouldn't he have called you?"

"My dear, you know him well, he's all business and no fun. Say this text again."

"*You will never find him, little signorina.*"

Uncle Lucio looked puzzled. "The sender wants you to worry. May I ask what you texted him first?"

"I asked him if he was okay, and I told him I was leaving . . . my mission. Alex would know it was from me."

"Any love words?"

"I said I loved him."

Uncle Lucio nodded, suddenly serious. "Alessandro . . . he was to pick up a contract yesterday, a big success for us, from the best winery in Abruzzo."

"He told me; he said it was one of his many problems."

"Hmm . . . maybe she's not harmless like I thought."

Her voice barely came out. "Who? Who's *she*?"

Lucio smiled and patted her shoulder. "Not to worry, *signorina*. This is not serious. Only a jealous woman."

22

A VOICE SHATTERS THE DARKNESS

In the back of the mafia van, Alex chafed and pulled at the cables on his wrists but the thugs who'd kidnapped him had pulled them tight. Fear flooded in when he realized they had to be ruthless criminals who killed easily. The ride was the longest of his life, wondering if they'd ever arrive. What was next?

Exhaust seeping inside the back door made him sick. The men talked in an unfamiliar dialect. Occasionally, he caught an Italian word, *castello* meaning castle and *Americano* more than once. They knew he was American, but would it afford him protective status or the opposite?

Early on he'd asked, "Where are we going?" only to receive a kick to his back that took his breath away. Then the guard pressed the cold metal of a gun against his chin.

"Shut up," he was told in Italian. No mouth gags were needed with those threats.

His acute sense of smell detected dried hay, sheep, and some kind of clay soil on the carpet. Any information he could pick up through his senses, he'd remember; it might save his skin. His hyper-vigilance was so strong he felt like screaming at every sound. How long had he been in this van? It seemed like a couple of hours already; it had to be dark outside.

At last someone opened the back of the van and pulled him and the others out, stumbling. The air was thin and breezy and didn't smell of plants, mostly of dirt. Gunfire startled him as it echoed through a valley. They had to be on top of a hill, where a Mafiosi fired a signal.

Someone grabbed him by the shoulders and he was told to walk fifteen steps, then thirty. *Snap*-his hands were released by a cut of the cable as he was shoved down on a gravel floor.

A door creaked shut and a lock clicked. Alex tore off the blindfold and blinked. He stood up, struggling against sore muscles. He was in a foul-smelling place where animals had been kept, a cave or a barn. He saw a dark figure in the shadows. "Marco? Are you here?"

"*Sì*, I'm here, *signore*."

"I am here, too," said the other man. "I'm Enrico."

"Call me Alex. Any idea why they kidnapped us?" Moonlight came from a small open window with bars on the top of a wooden door. The place was like a cave.

"You're the *Americano* they've been talking about," Enrico said, looking Alex over. "We must be careful, gentlemen, we've been captured by Camorra."

"Don't speak too loudly," said Marco, "the guards listen. My father also was kidnapped by them. He survived, and so will we, but we must be smart. Smarter than they are."

"They'll ask for ransom money, won't they?" Alex asked in a low voice.

"*Sì*, from our employers, our families." Marco seemed confident he knew what the Camorra were all about.

Enrico sounded scared. "So will they kill us if they don't get enough money?"

Marco answered, "*Sì*, but they may do something else with him."

"Did you see the guy in the sunglasses? Name was Casalesi." Alex barely whispered as they all did.

"Are you sure about that?"

"Casalesi, yes." Alex was certain.

"*Mamma mia*, it was Gianni Casalesi, the leader of the Camorra."
Marco pointed at Enrico. "With your fancy cars, they think you two are
very rich."

"My car is a blue heap of metal and it belonged to my uncle's business.
We're not rich, especially now," Alex said.

"Ah . . . your uncle will pay ransom." Marco sounded sure.

"He doesn't have much money," said Alex, his voice sinking.

"He must find it somehow. But the mafia has no use for me," said
Enrico, "I am only a lawyer in a hired car on my first trip to Abruzzo
from Rome."

Alex said, "I wouldn't think they like lawyers much."

"No, they kill them, unless . . . they have connections." Marco the
truck driver implied he knew everything. There's one in every group,
thought Alex.

"Connections you say? Hmm, I have a few. I may be able to get myself
out of here after all." Enrico's white smile shone in the moonlight. Alex's
distrust of the two men grew. Who knows how they were networked into
all of this?

"What do you mean, able to get yourself out?" Alex was incensed at
the thought they might get out and he couldn't.

"I mean, of course, there are ways to make deals with them from the
inside."

"Dangerous ways," Marco said, "but the *Americano* is right, they don't
like lawyers."

Enrico was unaffected. "I have no worries I will be freed soon."

Marco snickered. "Ah . . . you do have a connection." The two men
were a bit too relaxed and talkative.

Enrico's white teeth flashed. "I have a way." Enrico's Ferrari wasn't
damaged at the concrete roadblock. Maybe that was part of the plan, too.

"If you get out, can you negotiate my release, too?" Alex was desper-
ate. "My uncle is Lucio Giovanini in Roma and my name is Alexander
Dante Ca . . ." He stopped, thinking he shouldn't reveal his surname. Not
to these guys.

"You know what we Italians say. For every Dante there's a Beatrice," said Enrico. "Is that the reason you want out of here so badly? You have a girlfriend?"

"*Si*," said Alex, wondering if he'd ever see her again. Both men made joking comments and Alex realized he shared a cage with enemies.

Determined not to speak, Alex rolled his blindfold into a thin pillow and scooped away rocks so he could lie down. He curled into a fetal position and closed his eyes. Italy's seamy underside bared its fangs, alerting him that he'd only experienced the best of Italy, the good life.

The whole scene drummed before him like rain, pounding images of blood, guns, and black masked faces. He'd seen his share of TV violence, but what had just happened was terrifying, like living inside a movie you didn't want to be in.

Jennalee would think he'd stood her up because of their argument. Or maybe she hadn't shown up either. He worried the mafia would hurt his uncles or cousins and he hated to be the cause of Uncle Lucio paying a ransom for him. Then there was the wrecked Maserati; not his fault, but . . . that beautiful car.

■ ■ ■

At dawn, he woke up wondering where he was. Stiff and cold, he stood and saw the huddled shapes of two men on the dank cave floor. He took a deep breath and surveyed his surroundings.

A wooden door had been fitted into the only opening to the jail cell, with a barred window to let in light. Traces of brick walls covered with mud indicated a man-made place, probably used for centuries as a sheep shelter or a farm's tool shed. Alex stretched his legs, peering into every corner, but found the back of the cave too dark to explore. The path there looked like it went further underground.

He spotted a bucket of semi-clean water and drank from it. Another rusty bucket for fouler purposes was parked in a far corner of the cave. He found a wooden chair, pulled it out, and sat in it, feeling halfway civilized again when he heard the other men stirring.

"*Buongiorno*," said Enrico, "today I get out of here."

Alex ignored him. If he got released that day, it *proved* he was a crooked lawyer mixed up with the mafia.

Marco grinned. "*Sì*, me too; what would they want with a truck driver?"

Alex couldn't trust Marco either. For one thing, he wasn't scared enough when men pointed assault weapons at him yesterday. Almost like he knew them . . .

Rats, he thought, he'd missed the bank loan signing the day he found Jennalee in front of the Pantheon. By the time he got there after chatting with Firenza, it was too late and the bank was closing. Would Lucio even *have* any ransom money?

At the time Alex had thought he'd simply go back and sign the papers. Now, when his life depended on it, there would be no money. His uncle would be charged an exorbitant price for his release and be forced out of business. Disheartened, he put his head in his hands.

Marco smiled a partial toothless grin. "Breakfast soon."

"How do you know?" Alex asked. For some reason the man angered him.

Marco shrugged. "I hear stories. My grandfather was captured. . ."

Yesterday it had been his father. Marco was a liar. The two of them were mafia accomplices. He knew it.

Sure enough, in a few minutes, keys jangled, a lock clicked, and the door creaked open. Black-masked men directed the lawyer and truck driver outside with their guns. Alex stood back and was thrown a loaf of bread in a plastic bag. A fresh bucket of water was set down hard, some splashing out, and the door slammed shut. He was alone.

Alex shook the bars of the window. He shouted to the wind until it occurred to him they would shoot him if he made trouble. Better to be alone and try to think this out.

Why hadn't he driven the old Fiat and worn jeans instead of a suit? His thin tailored suit pants wouldn't hold up to this dirty place. He almost wished he hadn't covered the wounded woman with his jacket. How cold would it get here?

He poured out his frustration in loud cries to God. Why would God allow this? Anger burned, toward the mafia, and even his uncle. His life spun out of control. He could be dragged out and killed or tortured at any moment.

After another two days and nights, with little water or food, a shivering and hungry Alex woke at predawn to the sound of a faraway rooster's crows and to the reality of his situation. He got on his knees, not knowing where to begin in reaching out to the Most High.

He'd been living the fast life of a cool young professional, ignoring God, not listening to the Holy Spirit's gentle nudges, not hanging out with other Christians. Maybe Jennalee was right and he was on the way to losing his faith.

As he knelt on the rock floor in the cold, a soft worship song played in his head, and Alex sang, ". . . if darkness overwhelms me, Jesus, your light will overcome . . ." He sang it over and over to the morning stars and it bolstered him not to fear.

God saw him in the dungeon as he sang, like he'd seen Peter before him. He laid on the dirt floor, flooded with all the wrongs he'd done, driven to repent. The last time he'd seen Jennalee, he'd been a jerk, not even listening to her. How could he have been so callous when he'd been so loving a year ago?

Alex felt the quiet presence of the Holy Spirit. "I don't deserve such a mighty God. I've been awful, Lord. I've chased after money more than after you. You tried to show me in First Timothy, and I . . . didn't want to listen. I'm sorry for everything, for wanting too much, for not being loving to Jennalee. Whether I go to college or not, whether I marry her or not, I just want to do what you want. From now on, I'm yours . . ."

He spent all day praying as his water ran out. Never had he done that before. He prayed for whoever came to mind and for his mom and Gabe. He forgave kids from grade school, and asked for healing for the hurt after losing his dad.

When the outpouring of his soul lulled, peace fell like a waterfall, and he no longer cared about the mafia, the wrecked Maserati, or even escaping. Where earlier in his solitary confinement, he'd only felt despair, he now had the surety of a God who was bigger than anything; He was the God of angel armies.

As he grabbed the window bars, he said out loud, "Help all the people looking for me. I'm lost without you, Jesus, and need your power to get through this. Speak, Lord, I'm listening."

He startled when a very close, young voice said in Italian, "You talk to Jesus, eh? You think he will answer you?" A child's laugh followed.

23

BEYOND RELIGION

"What your father told me was someone tried to kill him," Brent said to Ammon after Otto woke up.

Ammon's brow furrowed. "It couldn't have been an accident. His job was one of the safest positions and I heard it happened in a section of the mine where he didn't even work."

"Well, someone has it out for him."

"And lured him to a different place in the mine?" Ammon sounded wary.

"Maybe. Didn't the doctors say it'll be a while before he can sort out his mind?"

"Right. It may be a while. No one knows how this head injury is going to affect him."

"I think he thought I was you, Ammon, and he only wanted *you* to know, nobody else."

"The doctors say his memory will come back in bits and pieces, so he's not totally coherent yet. Still, his color's back, he's eating real food. I think he's going to make it."

"I prayed for him to be healed, Ammon. And . . . his eyes opened." Brent watched for his friend's reaction. He hoped Ammon wouldn't disapprove.

"What? You didn't tell me this before."

"I didn't want you to think it was me. I've never prayed that way before; I had help from Rachel in Portland; we prayed together and it happened. He woke up."

Ammon looked at his friend with puzzled awe. "You've changed, Brent. You're like a new person."

Brent nodded.

"I wish I was in the place you're in; I need time to figure some of this out. I wanted to go back to the university so bad. They're holding my scholarships for me."

"Why can't you go? Your dad will be on disability; maybe your mom can get another job."

Ammon smiled, but his eyes were sad. "Because of debt. My dad owes everyone. How can I study knowing they'll take my family's house away?"

Brent saw for the first time how much Ammon's economic status would hold him back. Maybe his whole life. He didn't know what to say. "I bet there'll be a way you can go later."

"Yeah, maybe. I have good news, well, sort of. The coal mine offered me my dad's position. Starting pay is so high I can't turn it down."

Ammon in a coal mine instead of college?

"When do you start?"

"Monday for training."

Now Brent was the one to sigh. They had both completed two years of college, and how unfair for Ammon not to be able to earn his degree; the guy was nerdy smart. But Ammon's life was spoken for from this point on.

Ammon's tone intensified. "Back to what my dad said. What if it's true? What should I do?"

"Listen, I'm on this, I've got your back. You need to write down every strange thing happening at work, especially what people say. My uncles have a law firm in Salt Lake, and after you gather evidence, I'll take it to them. Keep a hidden folder at home, only be careful at work."

"I don't know if I can get much evidence, but I'll try."

"It could be a way out of this mess, Ammon, if it goes to court and you win the case."

A tiny smile appeared on Ammon's face, his eyes not so sad. His friend couldn't be called handsome, but he had an honest, pure look about him.

"I don't know what I would've done without you, Brent. At least *you* can go back to college next semester."

Ammon was selfless, he just was. It cut Brent to the core that this had happened to him.

"I could've ended up with the worst missionary companion ever, but you and I . . . we're like blood brothers, you know?"

"We are, and I have to . . . I need to tell you . . . don't leave the Church, Brent. I mean, I understand your doubts, but . . . you'll lose everything you've gained if you leave."

"I hear you. But you know my whole story; all the wrestling I did with doctrines and the Church's history."

"I thought you'd get over it when you came home."

"Ammon, I can't play the game anymore . . . but I'll always stick by you."

"Me, too, Brent."

■ ■ ■

All week, Brent stayed on the couch at Ammon's house with its dark sadness. While Ammon was at work, he went to the hospital to be with Otto, who was fighting a respiratory infection and still couldn't speak much.

The local ward poured food out for the Carr family, casseroles and trips to the bishop's pantry. He saw how good they were, his LDS people, and felt strange about being on the outside. But he was free and he wanted to practice it, even if it felt uncomfortable. After a while, the town began to depress him.

Instead of texting, he called Rachel one day. After that they talked or Facetimed every day. She knew why he was helping Ammon and she wanted to help, too.

"I'm leaving soon for my YWAM mission," she told him. "After I get back, think about coming to Portland to finish your degree. Only if everything's okay with Ammon, though. "

All during his mission, he'd missed his home. But Utah seemed different now, less like home. Maybe a new place would do him good, and he wanted to see if he and Rachel could make a go of it, long-term.

The couch got lumpier after he decided to leave Price. One restless night, as Brent formulated in his head how he was going to tell Ammon he was leaving the next day, he slipped off his shirt to change to a T-shirt.

"Brent? I was wondering if . . ." said Ammon, suddenly coming into the living room from upstairs. He wheeled around. No shirt, but worse, no sacred undergarment.

Ammon stood frozen in his tracks, frowning. "You're not wearing your garments."

He didn't want to apologize, but could feel Ammon's disapproving glare on his bare chest.

"No, I'm not." He shrugged and put on his T-shirt.

"Why? What does this mean, Brent?" Ammon's reproach hung between them.

"It means I can't. Even though the last thing my mom said was to keep wearing them, I have to tell you, they were the first to go." Facing the bishop had been hard, but facing Ammon was harder.

His friend's lips tightened into a thin disgusted line. "You know you have to dispose of them rightly. Where are they?"

"Don't worry, I kept the emblems." Brent reached into his jeans pocket and pulled out tiny cut-out markings, the embroidered sacred symbols that had been sewn on his under garments. "I'll just carry them around for a while and dispose of them like I'm supposed to."

"I didn't want to believe it . . . but you really are apostate. How can you expose yourself to danger like this, Brent? Without wearing your garments anything can happen."

"Ammon, I feel safer than I've ever been. Hey, something could happen to me, garments or not."

"But what about your sacred vows at the temple?"

"I don't want to make trouble with anyone," he said, "I just couldn't wear them anymore. I'm the same person, only closer to the true Jesus than I ever thought possible."

Ammon scowled. "I think you'd better go home tomorrow. I can't deal with this on top of everything else."

"It's okay. I was just going to tell you the same thing. Anyway, I'll be of more use to you presenting your dad's case to my uncles' law firm in Salt Lake. Even if I leave, Ammon, I'll always be your friend. And maybe someday you'll understand me better."

Ammon softened a little. "Thanks, Brent."

"Promise me you'll be careful on your job. It could be dangerous."

His friend nodded, and he watched as the new coal miner went upstairs, exhausted. Rolling over on the couch, he clutched his phone and read a text from Rachel.

> How's Ammon? I'm so ready! I'm going to Italy. Alison's going back to Argentina. I'll miss her. Like I told you, I won't be in Portland for three months, but I'd love it if you came for a visit. Or for college. God bless you, Rachel

So Rachel would be in Italy, where Jennalee was. He wrote a 'thank you' for the stacks of worship music she sent him and told her he'd talk to her about Ammon. He told her he'd meet her plane in Portland as soon as it came in. Three months to wait, or so he thought. How could he know that within hours his plans would change in in a drastic way?

24

FREEDOM GAINED

Brent almost fell off Ammon's couch reaching for his buzzing phone in the darkest hours of the night. Had to be an emergency. He blinked at the bluish light: his mother in Kaysville.

"Brent, sorry to wake you but I got a call from Jennalee's mission President in Italy. Your dad's on business in Nevada, and . . ." Her voice broke. "I don't know who else can help me."

"Has something happened to her? Is she okay?"

"She's disappeared; no one knows where. Her companion says she has an Italian boyfriend and she's been sneaking out at night. Rebellious. She's always been."

Here she goes again, he thought. His sister was far less rebellious than he was.

"It'll be okay, Mom. When are you going to tell Dad?"

"I didn't want to call and spring it on him tonight. He's had it rough lately."

He knew his dad was still upset at him because of the trouble he'd caused. Maybe he could make up for it and help him now.

"Brent, even if you aren't with us anymore, and even if you don't love us. . ."

He expected this. "C'mon, Mom. You know that's not true. Hey, this is about Jennalee. If you want me to go to Italy and find her, I will." He wanted to see her anyway; he hadn't seen her in two years.

A pause on the other end of the line. "Will you? You're the only one who's free to do this. When I tell your father, I know you'll go up a few notches in his book."

Exasperated, Brent said, "Maybe, Mom, but I know Dad's pretty mad at me. I'll find her, but I'm not promising anything. She might not want to come home."

"As long as she's safe, I'll be thankful. There must be some weakness in us because all these trials are happening. I don't understand why you kids are . . . going off like this. We used to be so blessed and happy."

"Okay, Mom, I'll drive to Salt Lake airport tomorrow and catch a flight out. I'll buy the ticket online tonight."

"I'll put some money in your account, son, and text you the mission President's number and address. I can break the news to your dad tomorrow." She paused. "Thank you."

"Remember I love you, Mom. Give hugs to the boys for me." He heard her crying on the other end of the phone before hanging up.

Jennalee . . . AWOL from her mission. Away Without Leave. Had she found Alex Campanaro? He lay on the couch, processing this. Jennalee was as loyal and steady as a golden retriever. It wasn't like her to run away from responsibility, no matter how their mom labeled her. Jennalee did think independently though, and he had to admit, he did, too. If it meant they went outside the rules, then so be it. But Jennalee might be in danger this time. In the darkness, he grabbed his phone and checked flights in the surreal blue light of its screen.

■ ■ ■

International flights excited him. Brent loved travel, especially to a place he hadn't gone before. He bought a quick Italian language app on the flight before landing at Fiumicino Airport, right outside the Eternal City of Rome.

Rome was like Argentina magnified with the number of churches he saw outside the window of the taxi. Nuns crossed the street in their black and white robes and veils. Priests conferred with one another on street corners. Rome was the heart of institutionalized Christendom but his own newborn Christian faith no longer centered on a Church, only a close relationship with Jesus. Maybe Rachel could help him find a good church to attend later. He knew he had a lot of questions for pastors.

Brent found the LDS office where his knock was answered by the mission President himself. A girl sat on a sofa with an older woman; the President's wife, he assumed by her nametag. "You must be Elder Young," said the girl whose badge said Sister McKay. She got up to shake his hand. "I know you're an RM, congratulations. I'm . . . well, I *was* Jennalee's missionary companion."

Brent winced a little at the titles clinging to him. They knew nothing about his doubts about the Church. He could play this game using prestige for an advantage, especially when he noticed the adoring face placing him high on the ladder of religious perfection. So he said, "Yes, Sister McKay, I'm a Returned Missionary. Okay, can you tell me who took my sister?"

"Elder Young, nobody *took* her. She ran away herself. I told her to stop, but she just kept running. She took clothes and stuff with her in a backpack."

"I see. You have a shared cell phone, don't you?"

"Yes, and she was texting on it and erasing them."

"May I see it? We all just want to find Jennalee and make sure she's safe, don't we?"

"I've been monitoring their phone," said the President, "if there's any evidence, I would've seen it. There was one text your sister said was a wrong number, but there are no unknown numbers in the phone. They are all LDS members or investigators. We have to send for the records to know more." He handed Brent the phone.

"So your LDS investigators are listed in here?"

"We didn't have too many because we just got here," said Sister McKay. He couldn't help but notice the President glance at her sideways.

Brent reviewed the contacts, which totaled six, including the mission President. One name stood above all the others: Alessandro Giovanini. He didn't know why the last name wasn't Campanaro, but it could be Alex. There weren't many calls, nor were they long. How could he find his sister with evidence this sparse? He memorized Alessandro's number anyway.

"What else can you tell me, Sister McKay?"

"All I know is I had to report her for sneaking out at night and kissing an Italian guy, one of our investigators; I know what I saw."

"What's his name?"

"Alessandro Giovanini."

Bingo, Alex alright. The girl chattered on, full of herself.

"He's a wine merchant, if you can believe it. Has a shop on the Via della Croce. Here, I wrote it down for you. Jennalee started talking to him about the church, then we both did. We only saw him once. This is so shameful. I can't believe what she . . ."

"You were going to refer this single guy to the elders, right?" He saw the mission President watching.

Sister McKay's eyes got large. "Of course, Elder Young. I hope you find her. Keep me posted; I care about your sister."

"Of course you do. And just so you know, I'm here representing my family, not the Church."

The President sneered a little. "I'm sure your family isn't too happy about your sister leaving her mission without a word to me. It's a scandal, that's what it is."

Brent had to take a deep breath to keep from physically settling the issue. "Scandalous or not, my sister, Jennalee *Young* may be in danger and that's why I'm here. My father's Stake President in Kaysville and my uncles have a law firm in Salt Lake so let's just say, I have a lot of back up."

The President bobbled his head in a slow nod and his wife stood next to him, reflecting her nervousness. "We hope you find her and will pray you do. If there's anything we can do, let us know."

■ ■ ■

Brent got on his smart phone and found the wine shop. Following an on-line map, he walked a mile to Via della Croce, where a freshly painted sign identified the Enoteca Giovanini, and he went inside. No one was behind the counter, but there was a noise in the back room. He rang the bell on the glass topped counter and he wasn't too surprised when his sister came out from a hallway in the back. When she saw him, she dropped the empty boxes in her hands.

"Hey, Sis. I came all this way to find you."

Jennalee hugged him tight. "Brent! I haven't seen you for two whole years," she said, almost starting to cry. They both talked at once when she took him by the shoulders, a serious look on her face.

"What's wrong?" he asked.

"Brent, you won't believe what's happened. I guess you figured out I found Alex. He was supposed to meet me and he wasn't there. He's miss-ing; something bad happened, I feel it."

"So this is why you left your mission?"

"Yes, because I need to find Alex. I suppose you met Sister McKay, and she told you the error of my ways. I did sneak out and meet him a couple times in secret."

"Don't worry, I figured it out."

"Brent, I don't have a testimony for the Church anymore. I know you disapprove and I have a lot to explain, but let's find Alex first."

"Hmm . . . have you thought about what you're doing, Jenn? I assume you know the consequences of your actions."

When he saw her bold expression waver, he felt sorry for her and broke into a grin. "Hey, Sis, we do need to talk . . . because I've changed just like you."

"So you're . . ."

"Jesus is more important than all the other stuff."

"I'm born-again, Brent. I can't say I'm not."

He nodded as she hugged him again. "Me, too. And there's more. Rachel, the girl who talked to me about Jesus is here in Italy with a Christian youth mission. After we find Alex, I hope to meet up with her."

Jennalee grinned. "So you had an ulterior motive. You didn't fly here for my sake."

"Well I did, but it's icing on the cake to see Rachel."

"I'll have to approve of this Rachel."

"No doubt about it, you'll love her."

"Okay," answered his sister, getting serious. "How much trouble am I in? Was the President angry? Are you going to tell him you found me?"

"Let's keep him at arm's length for a while. The Church isn't our priority but we do have to call Mom. She's the one who sent me here to find you. She was so upset she was crying, Jenn. Our parents are mad at us, but they love us . . . in their way."

"I love them, too, only I'm not going back yet. I have to find Alex first."

"And I'll help. Guess we're both AWOL, but at least we're in this together."

"Like old times when we were kids," she answered, "only different because we have Jesus."

25

THE POWER OF HIS NAME

"Who's out there?" Alex peered out of the barred window to see who was behind the little voice. A skinny boy with a dirty face jumped up in front of his window. A glimpse of brown hair sprouting from the top of his head made Alex think he'd seen this boy before.

"I am Fuglio, not Jesus," said the boy, backing up from the door so Alex could see him. "You pray very funny."

"Nice to meet you, too, Fuglio. I'm Alex. Hey, I've seen you somewhere before."

"My uncle says I cannot talk to you, only give water."

The boy took a plastic bottle of water from a bag and hoisted it up to the window. Alex put his arm down through the bars and took the bottle, almost dropping it before getting it back into his prison. "*Grazie,* I need water, but what about food? Does your uncle feed his prisoners? There *are* more prisoners around here, aren't there?"

The boy didn't answer, but Alex noticed him glance to his right before he handed Alex another water bottle.

"So you guys have another prisoner over there, huh?"

Fuglio grinned a gapped smile.

"Hey, you're the first person I've seen in days. How old are you?"

The boy held out ten fingers. "You wish," said Alex, "but you're six, maybe seven."

"How do you know, smart *Americano*?"

"Easy. Your two front teeth are missing." Fuglio closed his mouth and cocked his head at him, his hair moving like a crest of feathers. Then he pushed a food bag up to the bars.

"You're too short for this job," said Alex as he grabbed the bag and pulled it through. "But thanks for coming; you have no idea how much food means to me. Hey, aren't you going to give any to the guy next door?"

"How you know there is another prisoner?"

"Coughing, that's how. Is he sick?"

Fuglio nodded his head.

"Tell your uncle to let me in his cell. I'm a pretty good doctor; I'll make sure he gets well if you give me the right medicine. Your uncle wouldn't want his prisoners to die. How would he collect the ransom money?"

The mischievous boy nodded.

"I won't get you in trouble or anything. Just put me in with the sick guy."

Fuglio turned his head from side to side, then walked out of sight in the direction of the other jail cell. Alex tried to keep the boy engaged. "Today's the day for me to help that guy. Get the keys and let me in there and I'll give you these." He held out his designer sunglasses. The boy snatched them like a raptor and disappeared. Alex shouted after him until he was hoarse, not expecting to hear a man answer.

"Who are you?" His neighbor's weak voice strained to be louder.

"Alex Campanaro, an American."

"I am Massimo Torano. I'm very sick, but I am happy to know you are there. I must go now." His voice faded. "But I am glad to hear you sing."

■ ■ ■

Alex resolved to plan an escape. He was sure his uncle would pay anything to redeem him, but it would save a lot of trouble if he could get out of here himself. He planned to run when Fuglio's uncle let him out and somehow, he'd help Massimo escape, too.

First, he'd assess everything in the cave he could use as possible tools. He had the chair and his blindfold. He kicked around the dust in the back of the dungeon in hopes a shepherd had left a sharp tool, and he found a broken knife blade, empty cans, and rat droppings.

The dark tunnel he'd noticed earlier bothered him, but it could be a way out. He needed to explore it. The steep grade made his leather soled shoes slip, and he fell, sliding through spider webs all the way down. He stood up and dusted himself off, glad his pants hadn't torn. Without light, he inched down, step by dark step, his hand on the damp wall. Rats and spiders weren't his favorite things.

After reaching what had to be the end of the tunnel, a bit of light wafted down from a crack in the rock in the ceiling; enough to see a wooden table with boxes under it. Unbelievable. Four crates of unlabeled wine, aging and forgotten were under the table. Alex took out a bottle, blew the dust off and worked out the cork with his knife blade.

Immediately the scent of an elegant wine overpowered his nostrils. He took a deep whiff. Orange overtones filled his olfactory, along with the scent of the oak casks that held the wine. For lack of a wineglass, he poured a little into his hand to see its dark red color in the dim light, then tasted it out of the bottle. Of the all official varieties of wine in Italy, this he could identify.

Rolling down his throat like velvet was the one-of-a-kind blue Aglianico grape in its fermented form. He'd tasted it once, in his uncle's villa. This wine was from Taurasi, a town in the Campania region. Those three hours blindfolded in the back of a van had transported him inland to a place where ruined medieval castles from the Normans and Lombards dotted the hillsides. The center of Camorra territory.

Carrying his opened bottle, he crawled back up the path to look outside with a new eye. Was his jail cell under a ruined *castello*? Had to be, since he was on a lonely outcropping above a valley where the wind spooked through old stones. Taurasi was somewhere below. Not only did he know where he was, but he now had a treasure. At seventy Euros a bottle, it could help him buy his way out.

26

PRAY ALWAYS

Right after Brent found Jennalee in the wine shop, Alex's uncle Lucio breezed through the front door, setting down a bag of bread, salami and cheese, and announced, "My car, my Maserati, has been found wrecked on the bottom of a hill in Abruzzo." He was so agitated Jennalee rushed over to him and put a hand on his shoulder.

"Where's Alex? Is he hurt?" Jennalee's face was so worried, Brent didn't know what to say.

"The *polizia* say Alex was not in the car; it was empty when hit, then rolled down the mountain."

Jennalee let out her breath, and Brent did, too.

Lucio made a wide sweeping gesture with his entire arm. "Ah . . . who is this? Your other boyfriend?"

Brent stepped up, knowing his sister was in no mood to joke around. "You must be Alex's uncle Lucio. I'm Brent Young, Jennalee's *brother*."

Lucio shook his hand with a firm grip. "All the way from America?"

Jennalee said, "He came to find me but now he has to help us find Alex . . . if he can forget his girlfriend Rachel's in Italy, too."

Lucio moaned. "If only you didn't have a girlfriend and were free, *Signore*. You see, I have three daughters."

Brent almost laughed. "Rachel's from America. I'll see her soon, she understands I'm busy."

"Okay, enough chit chat," said Jennalee, intensely staring at Uncle Lucio. "Now tell us everything you know. Where was Alex if he wasn't in the car?"

Lucio went back to obsessing about the Maserati. "There were people who saw Alex help the woman who hit . . . my car. Then he disappeared."

Jennalee sighed. "He's in trouble. We'd better go help him, like now."

"We will drive to Abruzzo to see the scene and ask around. Ah, but I am worried about you, my tired friend from America. Perhaps you should stay upstairs. We have two beds up there and a cot. Not so comfortable, the cot . . ."

"But the beds are wonderful," said Jennalee.

Brent laughed again. "Are you kidding? Forget it, I'll just get a shot of espresso. I had one on the plane." The shock on Jennalee's face was worth it.

"Your sister won't touch coffee," Lucio said, "how is it you are from the same family and not Mormon?"

"I am, but it's too complicated to explain," he said, noticing his sister's anxious face. "We better go, I'll sleep in the back seat."

Uncle Lucio mumbled, "I never understand about you Mormons and coffee and wine . . . what kind of life is it without coffee and wine?" He shook his head.

"Wait, Lucio. Did you call Alex's mother?" asked Jennalee.

"*Si*, I talked to my sister. Gina's the religious one, so she prays about this. She cannot come home to Italy, so I keep her up to speed, is how you say?"

Brent saw Jennalee getting more and more undone. "Let's go find him, then," Jennalee said, practically stamping her foot.

"*Si*, there is no sense staying here," said Lucio, grabbing the bag of food. He zipped the shop shutters down, locked it and they piled into a small Fiat parked in front. Brent stretched out as best he could in the back seat. As if he could sleep with all of this, he thought.

He saw buildings fade away as they left Rome and long-needled pine trees take their place.

Jennalee spoke. "Uncle Lucio, I think Alex was unsettled about going to Abruzzo. He didn't say why. Do you have any ideas?"

"Perhaps it was something about Largo and Caprice Putifaro, who have the best vineyard in Abruzzo. I think they give my poor son a hard time about signing a contract."

"I don't know why he didn't want to go."

"I should have gone with him," answered Lucio.

"May I ask you if . . . Alex had other girlfriends, you know, like Firenza."

"Firenza?" Uncle Lucio guffawed. "Ah . . . *bella*. It would be a good match, of course, with all her money. . ."

"Lucio! Watch out!" Jennalee shouted as he steered the tiny car too close to the guard rail at top speed. Brent had to hold on as he swerved back on to the highway.

"I am in complete control of the car. You will not worry with me behind the wheel," said Lucio, feigning hurt. All Brent could think of was what his parents would do if two of their children were in a car accident in Italy.

"Want me to drive?" he asked Lucio.

"No, no. I just had a thought; that's all." Then silence.

Jennalee said, "Aren't you going to tell us?"

"I wonder if this could be . . . Camorra." He whispered the word and Brent saw color drain from his cheek.

"I'm sorry, what?" Jennalee asked.

Brent blurted out, "You mean he's been kidnapped by the mafia, don't you?" Even as he said it, a wave of shock hit him.

Lucio nodded. Jennalee froze, looking terrified.

"Shouldn't we get help from the police?" Brent asked. He kept an eye on the road to brace himself if Lucio went off again. As if he could save himself; maybe Ammon was right and he shouldn't have taken his garments off after all, he thought with irony.

Lucio shrugged. "We Italians don't like to talk about mafia but there are rumors Camorra has been warned by the government to stop trying to gain control of the wine industry. Me, I wish to have a clean export business; no Mafiosi is going to fool with me or my nephew."

Brent whistled. "Sounds like they are fooling with you now. I think we should call the police as soon as we get there."

"Tsk, tsk. You Americans don't understand. The *polizia* . . . I'm afraid they cannot be trusted."

"So what are we going to do?" asked his sister.

"We must find people and ask what they see and hear that day. But it is time for lunch as you call it."

"We have food, let's keep going until we get to the scene of the wreck," said Brent.

He ignored him. "I treat you to pizza; the first one *Signore* has had in Italy," he said, taking the next exit ramp. The man was exasperating, and Brent began to think they could do more without him.

Still, he'd never tasted pizza like the one in the little café they stopped at. Lucio asked the waitresses, and any townspeople hanging around outside about the accident. Brent could tell they knew something but weren't talking. One woman whispered, "Camorra . . ." and then slipped away.

Lucio explained. "It is an honor code in this village. They know, but they do not talk."

"We're not going to find anything this way. So the mafia is accepted around here, like spaghetti?" Jennalee said.

Lucio smiled. "Like spaghetti, *Signorina,* all those strings. Most of us don't ever see mafia, but Camorra, Cosa Nostra, Ndrangheta . . . they all are stronger in our bad economy. They, how you say, shake down good people for money. Where there is money, there is mafia."

His shoulders sagged. "Giuseppe warned me when I started the business. What have I done? I sent Alex out into this world before he is ready." Brent heard genuine sorrow in Lucio's voice.

They came to a winding piece of road and they saw it. The blue Maserati had landed on its side on a slope of trees and brush. Lucio screeched his brakes and parked the Fiat at an angle on the side of the road. He leaped out and went over to his car, as if it were a dead relative, shaking his head in lamentation.

A tow truck was backed up to the crushed car. Brent and Jennalee got out and stood a near it to watch.

Brent said, "So tell me, is Lucio crazy or is it just me?"

"He's a little eccentric, but it's your first day in Italy and you have culture shock."

"I'd say it's just shock." They watched as tow truck man righted the Maserati with a hook and a thud.

Lucio came over to them, shaking his head. "We have insurance, of course, but such a car I'll never have again." In rapid Italian, he spoke to the man in charge for several minutes.

Pacing, Lucio made his way back to them. "The driver, he notices mystery wrecks often in these hills. He says they are caused by Camorra who block the road. He is afraid, so I slipped him some money and he talked."

"Did he see Alex?" asked Jennalee.

"He says a shepherd saw armed men put three prisoners in a white van. One of the kidnapped fits the description of our own dear boy. No one killed. The shepherd said the white van took a side road and went south. How far? Anyone's guess." Lucio's hands moved with every word he spoke.

"Won't they want money for Alex?" Brent asked. "They should be calling you soon." Seeing the crunched blue Maserati and knowing Alex had been in it moments before impact was hard for Jennalee and he put an arm around her.

"I hear not a word from them on our business phone," answered Uncle Lucio. "They give me the ruined laptop. I throw it in the woods, but here is his briefcase." He snapped it open and inspected the Putifaro papers. An iPad was in there, too.

Lucio said, "My sister Gina doesn't like the Putifaros. She worries about Alex and about that woman, Caprice."

"What do you think happened?" asked Brent.

"You see, Caprice likes young men, but she is twenty years too old for them. Her husband pays no attention. He is old and fat."

Jennalee was visibly upset. "Alex never said anything to me about her, but he was worried about work. He said he might have made an enemy. What if a jealous husband has done this?"

Lucio shook his head. "Largo is not so jealous to do this."

Brent spoke up. "Let me get this straight. This Caprice lady likes young guys like Alex and he was coming here to sign a contract? She's a cougar, and not even from BYU."

Jennalee rolled her eyes. "I'm sure Alex is innocent of anything wrong. I know him."

"Have you heard the saying, *'hell has no fury like a woman scorned'*?" Brent asked.

"*Sì*," Lucio said in a low voice, "we have a similar saying. It could be true in this situation."

"Maybe the Putifaro vineyard is involved with the mafia," said Jennalee, "and Camorra didn't want Alex's deal to go through."

Lucio's brows crossed in worry. "If the Putifaro vineyard is allied to them, we better not go there. It could be a trap."

"Why can't we bring in the police?" Brent asked. To him, rule of law would have to apply, even to the mafia.

Lucio shook his head. "You Americans. The *polizia* will not go with you. To them, all we can do is report him missing. This is a job for the *carabinieri*."

"*Carabinieri*? Another police force?"

"*Sì*, the *carabinieri* are military, never working in the province where they are from for safety reasons. If the kidnappers call me then I call the *carabinieri*. Not that anyone wants to fight against Camorra, but there are a few brave *carabinieri*."

Jennalee looked baffled. "Every country has its quirks, I guess."

"Quirks? What is this word?"

"It means weirdness."

Lucio's blank face told them he didn't understand, but he just shrugged. Brent spoke decisively. "We need a plan to rescue him, even if it's only us against the mafia."

"Tsk, tsk. My dear Youngs," said Lucio, "we can only wait. My brother Giuseppe is seeing a lawyer today and will put money in the bank for ransom. Do not try anything by yourselves. It's too dangerous. How do you Americans say it? It's like looking for a needle in a hay bale."

Brent tried to hide his grin and said, "Strategy is everything. What do you think about this plan? You go back to Rome, Lucio. Talk to the ones who listen, the *carabinieri*. Wait for the kidnappers to call. My sister and I will stay here and pose as tourists to find information. Someone around here knows where Alex is."

Lucio reached into his jacket and gave them a roll of Euros. "You're right, I can do no more here. If you stay, you need bribes. And remember, the people of Abruzzo like Americans, but you're in danger. Be careful who you talk to."

"Alex needs us. We don't care about the danger." Jennalee said.

■ ■ ■

Lucio rode them in the Fiat to the next village where a sign posted scooters for rent. Brent actually bought a scooter at a high price. When Lucio drove off, both of them let out long sighs of relief.

"Well, Sis, we're on our own." Brent was feeling tired now.

"Police report first, I don't care. Maybe they know something."

He shrugged. "I can't argue with you and win."

At the station, the police officers were so laidback, Brent wondered if they were even working. How could real police be so nonchalant about a missing American? Two officers switched to a regional dialect so he and Jennalee couldn't understand them, but he thought they grumbled about Americans ordering them around. They ogled his sister so much, what would've happened if Jennalee had been alone?

"I thought Lucio said they like Americans," Jennalee said when they went outside.

"They liked *you* so much, I was going to set them right. But then I thought being in jail wouldn't help our cause."

"I kind of thought they might grab me, too."

"Creepy. We might be in over our heads here, Jenn."

"Let's stay away from the police." Jennalee grinned. "In all of this, Brent, I'm so happy you came to find me."

"I am, too. I was up for an adventure now that I'm free."

"I'm feeling guilty leaving my mission. Our poor parents. I know God sent you here to give me courage, Brent."

"You did the right thing to leave. It's more important to find Alex. We'll take care of your mission prez and official stuff after all this is over."

"So have you left the Church?"

"I'm wondering how . . . I mean, it's harder than I thought. You don't just leave."

Jennalee took a deep breath. "You're not wearing your temple garments."

"How can you tell?"

"The sleeve line under your shirt is missing . . . the thickness around the chest isn't there."

"Caught again. I couldn't wear it any more. Ammon totally disapproved when he found out, but I think we're still friends."

"I guess he can't understand, and I'm not totally there yet myself." Jennalee grinned with mischief in her face. "Hey, Brent, since Rachel's in Italy, too . . ."

"Rachel is busy and if I learned anything on my mission, it was patience. Jennalee, I came over here for you . . . and to meet the guy you left your mission for."

"Which I should've done a long time ago."

"Why didn't he tell you more about this contract with Putifaros?"

"I don't know. He was keeping secrets but I know he wouldn't have gone over to the mafia's side, and he wouldn't have done anything improper with Caprice Putifaro; who I need to talk to, by the way."

"Oh no, you don't."

"Why not?"

"Here's what I think. She may have gone after Alex and if he's the guy you say he is, he told her *no*. In which case, she whistled for the Camorra guys to, I don't know . . . punish him."

"But they took *three* men captive in the white van."

"Maybe it was an opportunity to collect more money; shake down rich guys. I think the main intent was to get Alex."

"It's a good theory, Brent. Alex was also picking up his cell and I think . . . could *she* have his phone?"

"If she does, we'll get it. No one knows who we are and we can investigate the Putifaros. They can't be any scarier than the police."

"Well they could be. Lucio said not to go near their place; it may be a mafia controlled trap, especially if Alex is there. Poor Alex. He might be tied up in some basement."

"Here's the plan. We go to the house as Mormon missionaries. Do they know missionaries aren't ever a man and a woman?"

Jennalee beamed at him. "No one knows anything about LDS here. Just a minute, I'll see if I can find my nametag." She dug in her backpack. "Here it is, and I know where the vineyard is because I saw it on the maps in Alex's briefcase. He'd circled it."

"Hm. I don't speak the language so I'll let you do the talking," said Brent, "but we have to get her guard down so we can search for the phone."

"What if Caprice slams the door in our faces?"

"She won't, not if she's the cougar I think she is." Brent had to laugh.

"You're going to be the bait?"

"I prefer the word decoy."

27

FORTRESSES FALL

Napping about noon, Alex woke when he heard his jail room being unlocked. He hoped they wouldn't notice how much he'd chipped at the door with his knife, hours of work that didn't make much of a dent. He felt no real fear.

In the door frame stood a graying man wearing a three piece suit.

"Get up," said the man, "come with me, Alessandro Campanaro. Your uncle is working with us."

Alex stood, tucking his shirt into his worn out pants. "Does this mean I'm free? Did my uncle pay my ransom?"

The man didn't answer but pulled him outside into the sun. He was unarmed and the only other person with him was a solemn Fuglio, whose eyes darted away from Alex's.

"Where are we going?" asked Alex.

"So untrusting, have we not taken good care of you?"

"No, not really. You have no right to hold me here against my will. Did you know I'm a citizen of the United States? I want to go to the Embassy."

"We do know this and you are a businessman, are you not?"

"I see you know all about me," Alex said. They walked around what was clearly a ruined Lombardy castle. Twenty feet from the cliff side jail cell where he was kept, another cell door was open. For a few seconds, they stood in front of it and a rush of adrenalin told Alex to make a break for it and run.

But he found he couldn't, not when he saw inside the cell. The young man lying on a cot inches off the ground, moaned in a low voice. The guy was too sick to move.

"This man needs your assistance," the man in the suit said in a grim tone. Then he shoved Alex with such power he stumbled and fell into the dismal cell.

The door slammed shut. So much for escaping. Alex rubbed his scuffed knees as he stood. "Massimo?"

"*Sì*," said a weak voice, "I thank God he sent you. I think I'm dying. A terrible weight sits on my chest."

Alex put his hands on Massimo's head. Hot. A fever raged so high he probably hallucinated.

"It's got to be pneumonia. We need get you out of here and get some antibiotics."

"I'm so weak I can't get up anymore to get water."

"You got it bad, but I'm not going to let you die. I know where we are; we'll get out somehow."

"*Grazie, amico*," said the thin young man, closing his eyes.

Massimo's fever raged and his hollow breathing disturbed Alex while he picked at the wooden door with the old knife blade he'd had in his pocket. At least he hadn't been searched. The captors had given them a bucket of water, and Alex bathed his friend's head with the blindfold he'd stuffed into his pocket.

This door frame was rotting away in strategic points so he applied the knife blade to it like a sculptor, using a rock to chisel off splinters of wood near the hinges. He sang worship songs for a couple hours as he whittled: ". . . nothing formed against me shall stand. . ."

Three hours later, with a small pile of wood chips around his feet, he looked outside the window. An eerie fireball blazed in the sky, pulsating in a curved arc, not far above where they were. He'd seen a TV show about weather phenomena, but he couldn't remember what this light was. Minutes later, the bright aurora trembled; the air was electrified.

Then, a rumble like a train coming full rush was followed by a jolt and shaking. He fell on the ground next to Massimo, who woke up with round eyes, afraid.

"*Terremoto!*" he said.

An earthquake. Alex stumbled to the window and saw a tree uproot and crash down the stony cliff with a roar. The door rattled so much he thought it might break. He kicked it with all he had, and it wavered, but didn't give. The light in the sky flashed and the earth heaved a strong shake from side to side. Splinters flew around him as the doorframe buckled, punching the door to the ground outside.

They were free. He spun around and scooped Massimo in a fireman's carry position. In spite of his name, the young man was not massive, but wiry and small. He found Fuglio, grimacing in fear, holding on to a sapling, his legs braced. Their food bags were on the ground beside him. Alex set Massimo on the grass and the three of them huddled as the shaking continued.

As they watched, a sudden jolt shook the castle. The stone walls shuddered, then plunged into a pile of white dust. The only part left standing was the area they'd just escaped from. Alex's old prison cell was crushed.

Fuglio let go of the tree and grabbed Alex's pants in a strong grip, with eyes full of fear. Massimo's gray face revealed what Alex already knew. Above all else, they needed a hospital.

28

FINDING ALEX

From the back of a motor scooter, the beauty of the countryside took Jennalee's breath away. Fields of ripe wheat, olive groves and vineyards flew past as she thought about how to find Alex. She'd crossed the river she never thought she could cross, only there was no Alex on the other side.

After a restless night in a tiny country inn, she and Brent were on their way to the Putifaro vineyard. Lucio called, saying there was no word from Camorra, but they didn't reveal to him where they were headed. She and Brent had planned and re-planned, but it made her heart beat fast when he pulled the scooter on to the long dirt road leading to the Putifaro's house.

A few grape harvesters raised their heads but went back to work without interest in them. The grounds around the house were deserted and the farmhouse itself not as grand as she thought it would be.

The porch floorboards creaked as they went up to the dusty door. They had no idea if their ruse would work, as they rang an outside bell at the door and waited. No answer. Brent rang again.

"Do you think this is the right house? The couple is rich, Alex told me, and this house . . . well, it's not what I thought it would be." It even felt spooky to her.

"Maybe this is their first place, the one they had before they were rich. Looks so old that maybe they inherited it. Anyway, there's no one here, or they're not answering."

"Brent, Alex could be locked up around here, in some deserted basement or attic."

"Let's investigate." They sneaked to the back porch and tried the door. It opened.

"Hello?" Brent called out. No one came, and they went inside.

"We shouldn't be in here. I have a bad feeling about this," she whispered.

"Stay with me," he said, leading her downstairs to a roughed-in basement, empty except for bottles and cobwebs. Nothing. Brent even went up the attic ladder and still no sign of Alex. They returned to the motorbike outside.

"Maybe he's tied up in the barn or those sheds over there. He could be anywhere." Jennalee began to panic. It was obvious no one had been here a long time. Except for the open door.

They searched the outbuildings. Nothing. "I need water," said Brent, heading back to the kitchen. Scared to stay outside alone, she followed him.

"You didn't find his phone, did you?" he asked, his face wet.

"No. She probably still has it. Where do you think they are?"

"They haven't been here for a while. I suppose we could ask the harvesters."

"Let's not, they may be mafia spies. But I wonder why the door was open."

"Who knows? Hey, I'm disappointed, I wanted to see that Caprice woman." Brent frowned. "Guess we better go to the nearest village and ask about the Putifaros." On their way out, the workers in the vineyard had disappeared.

"Quitting time, I guess," Brent said.

"Something's weird around here," his sister answered, "they must be scared or something."

"Or something. I wonder if they left to warn the Putifaros."

They ended up at a café which turned out to be the village's social center. Jennalee chatted with the mustachioed owner, asking about the famous Putifaro wines.

"Let's see, aren't the owners Caprice and her husband, Largo?" she asked sweetly.

He was evasive, telling her in a low tone, "We don't talk about them here. Caprice Putifaro was born a Casalesi."

"Her maiden name?"

The owner nodded. "Did you hear me? Casalesi. You are American and don't know how dangerous it is to ask questions about the family. Find the name on his fancy phone. C-a-s-a-l-e-s-i. I will say no more."

Jennalee nodded in silence and bowed her head a bit. "Give me your phone," she ordered her brother. He handed it to her, with a sharp look. She googled the name and saw the webpage confirming the name of the leaders of the Neapolitan mafia, Camorra.

Jennalee realized how horribly serious this all was. "Naples is three hours from here and it's probably where the white van went. Didn't the shepherds say it went south? That's probably where the Putifaros went, too."

"So you want to head south?" Brent shook his head. "Where? It's like finding a needle in a hay bale."

"Very funny, Brent. I have no idea but I'll figure it out. Hand me the map."

Brent ate their last slice of pizza as a TV droned on in the background, announcing soccer scores. Brent nudged her arm as he watched TV; the soccer show had been interrupted with a news bulletin.

"There's been a bad earthquake," he said.

In Italian, a reporter began, "An hour ago, the Prime Minister of Italy declared a state of emergency in the area of Taurasi, Avellino province, the epicenter of a 7.4 earthquake. The death toll is at ninety-eight; a number likely to rise. With homes destroyed and fearing aftershocks, hundreds are on the streets. This is Silvestro Icarino from the BBC, reporting at the Croce Rossa clinic in Taurasi." The camera swung around to film chaos and knee-high stony rubble in the streets.

Jennalee covered her mouth with her hands. Behind the reporter were two faces, both young men, one with wild hair and a week old beard. Even in the two seconds she saw him, she knew it was Alex. Blood was on his face and he held up another man with his arm. A dirty little boy gripped his pant leg.

"Brent, it's him," she yelled. "Do you see him? It's Alex."

"You mean you saw him in the earthquake report?"

Her eyes glued, she scanned the TV screen for any other sign of him. The reporter talked to a number of people in shock, and there were more camera shots of rubble and falling buildings. Then the news report cut off abruptly and Jennalee ran up to the counter.

"Scusi, where was the earthquake, where did they film?" she begged the café owner. "I missed the name."

"Taurasi," he said, "in Campania, south of here, but you are crazy to go there. And there are aftershocks. The quake in L'Aquila was like this . . ." He shook his head.

Alex was in Taurasi, hurt, but walking. "Was it a hospital where they filmed?"

"The Red Cross Clinic; it's all they have in Taurasi. *Signorina,* you did not see the running news tape at the bottom? After they film, the building behind the BBC journalist collapsed and he was killed. I hope you did not know him."

No, she thought, not him, but I know . . . the man behind him. Nothing would stop her now. She would find Alex.

End of Book Two
To be continued in *For Time and Eternity*
Believe in Love Series, Book Three

Sources:
"Out of the Wreck I Rise", chapter heading from a poem by Robert Browning
LDS Hymn, "Praise to the Man", words by William W. Phelps, 1792-1872, Music: Scottish Folk Song

ACKNOWLEDGEMENTS

I thank Jesus for meeting me 37 years ago in Italy and for allowing me to live in Utah for several years. What I feared would hinder spiritual growth became a catalyst for renewal. By making me a stranger in a different religious culture, I was given a springboard to write about authentic relationship with God.

In Utah, I befriended a number of wonderful people who I wanted to talk to about my relationship with the Biblical Jesus. Those discussions never happened and to get them out of my head, I wrote this series. What better way to show truth in love than through a love story?

Although I've attempted to relay the LDS experience to the best of my ability, I rely on research and the varied backgrounds of people who grew up LDS, as I did not. The story is for all seekers of a closer relationship with God than any religious institution can provide.

In writing *A Saint in the Eternal City*, I'm grateful for the invaluable help of Jeanie Jenks, Julie Hymas, Barbara Heagy, Emma Hofen, Lindy Jacobs, Yvonne Kays, Julie Johnson and my husband, Ray Croft. Also, Lynn Wilder's biographical book, *Unveiling Grace*, profoundly affected me with the heroic story of her family's journey to recognize the true Jesus.

For readers of my first book, *A Gentile in Deseret*, who have waited so long for this sequel, thank you for your understanding; I'm profoundly sorry for the delay in publishing *A Saint in the Eternal City*.

ABOUT THE AUTHOR

 Rosanne Croft is the author of *A Gentile in Deseret*, and *A Saint in the Eternal City*, Books 1 and 2 of the Believe in Love series. She co-authored *Once upon a Christmas*, a 2015 nationwide bestselling Christmas short story book published by Shiloh Run Press, an imprint of Barbour Books. Her other credits include co-authoring the historical novel, *Like a Bird Wanders*, and contributions to *What Would Jesus Do Today? A One-Year Devotional*, by Helen Haidle. Residing near Bend, Oregon, Rosanne is an active member of Oregon Christian Writers and Central Oregon Writers Guild. She loves to write, teach sewing and have tea with friends.

See her blog at www.rosannecroft.wordpress.com.